Stories from the Hearts
of Two Grandmas

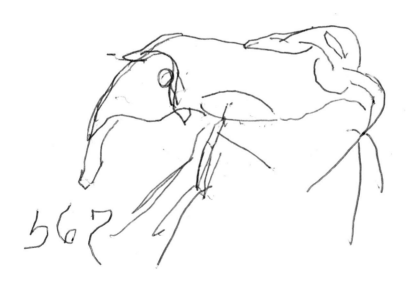

Stories from the Hearts of Two Grandmas

Ibbie Ledford
Johnnie Countess

PELICAN PUBLISHING COMPANY
Gretna 1998

Copyright © 1997
By Ibbie Ledford and Johnnie Countess
All rights reserved

First printing, 1997
Second printing, 1998

The word "Pelican" and the depiction of a pelican are trademarks of Pelican Publishing Company, Inc., and are registered in the U.S. Patent and Trademark Office.

Library of Congress Cataloging-in-Publication Data

Ledford, Ibbie.
　Stories from the hearts of two grandmas / Ibbie Ledford and Johnnie Countess.
　　p.　cm.
　Includes index.
　ISBN 1-56554-214-2 (pbk. : alk. paper)
　1. Grandmothers—Tennessee—Biography. 2. Tennessee—Biography. 3. Conduct of life. 4. Ledford, Ibbie. 5. Countess, Johnnie. I. Countess, Johnnie.
CT261.L43　1996
　976.8'05'092—dc20
　[B]　　　　　　　　　　　　　　　　　　　　96-27456
　　　　　　　　　　　　　　　　　　　　　　　　CIP

Manufactured in the United States of America
Published by Pelican Publishing Company, Inc.
P.O. Box 3110, Gretna, Louisiana 70054-3110

To our grandchildren (Johnnie's Sara and Mark; Ibbie's Will, Tray, Deidra, and Steve) and to our children who gave us our "Grands" (Johnnie's Elaine and Brenda; Ibbie's Tim, Steve, and Debby). To Mama and Papa, who not only gave us physical life, but taught all ten of their children the all-important values of honesty, hard work, and respect for themselves and others. To our six brothers, two sisters, and to our husbands (Johnnie's Tom and Ibbie's Willie); and to our Aunt Ibbie and Uncle John who helped raise us, and for whom we are named. Without our families who gave us the material for Stories from the Hearts of Two Grandmas, *we would not have stories to tell.*

And a special dedication to our brother, Pfc George Wallace Lock, killed in action in the performance of his duty and service to his country, on Paulau Island, October 4, 1944.

Contents

Introduction 9

Chapter 1	The S.O.G. Club (Silly Old Grandmas) 13
Chapter 2	About Parents 27
Chapter 3	Love and Marriage 53
Chapter 4	This and That 63
Chapter 5	Live and Learn (Bits of information learned from our combined 126 years of living) 97
Chapter 6	We're Thinking 123
Chapter 7	A Bit of History (Our brother's experience in the Gulf War) 135
Chapter 8	Christmas Memories 139
Index	155

Introduction

We are sisters in our sixties who persistently proclaim, "It's a wonderful life," and our stories reflect that feeling. We believe that laughter is a very important part of life. How else could we cope with life's aggravations and disappointments? And then there are times when it feels good to shed a tear or two. We laugh, we cry, and life goes on, and is good.

Writing has proven to be therapeutic and rewarding for us, and helps us maintain and enjoy a close relationship. The nostalgic stories bring back pleasant memories, and stories of the present keep us aware of life's changes. We hope your emotions will be stirred as you read our stories. If so, it will prove them worthy of your time and make us very happy.

Stories from the Hearts
of Two Grandmas

Chapter 1

The S.O.G. Club
(Silly Old Grandmas)

I'M A PROUD MEMBER OF THE S.O.G. CLUB
by Johnnie

His three-and-a-half-foot frame was dwarfed as he stood gazing up at the huge Ferris wheel. His fine, blond hair blew in the warm breeze. His eyes were as black as coals and shone like diamonds. He talked loud and fast, trying hard to control his excitement, a smile all over his face. That smile warmed my heart. It was the smile of my first grandchild.

The fair was moving in, and though Markie was only four years old, this was the third year that the fair held special fascination for him. I don't know how he did it, but he knew when the very first truck pulled onto the fairgrounds, even though we lived clear across town. Every year on Labor Day weekend we would make several trips to watch the fair make preparations. The rides were set up and the animals brought in, which Markie enjoyed most of all, though he thought they sure did smell.

On this particular outing, as I watched Markie standing there so tiny beside the big wheel, my heart bursting with pride, I whispered a prayer as I often do, that God would always hold him in His hand.

It's funny how a grandchild never needs scolding or spanking. Elaine says, "But Mother, you spanked me!"

"You needed it. Markie doesn't," I explain.

A grandchild keeps one young. Markie wouldn't believe me if I told him I was too old to play chase, so I would play chase; and, by golly, I wasn't too old! When he would see a stooped, gray-haired old man, he'd begin to worry that his granddad, Daggie, would someday get old. He would say, "Daggie, promise me you'll never get old."

Markie would light up a room simply by being there. He often dressed up like a ghost, putting a white handkerchief around his face and swooping down on us, scaring us as he intended. For a few brief moments we would enter once again the exciting, make-believe world of a child.

His four-year-old logic never ceased to amaze me. At one end of the midway was a scary-looking ride. A big, devil-like creature dominated the front, with the sign saying Ride with the Devil.

"What's it say, Gran?"

I read it aloud. "Not me," said Markie. "I'm not riding with no debal."

He would keep us when his parents went out. He'd say, "Gran, I like staying with you. It's fun coming to your house." That would be music to any granny's ears.

Most baby-sitters get paid, but when his parents come to get Markie, I ask how much I owe them for the pleasure of his company. Never mind that he painted my mailbox purple, nor that he used my king-sized bed for a trampoline.

It is true that grandparents fill a special need for their grandchildren, but the child fills a much bigger void in us. Markie would enter my quiet home like a whirlwind, leaving it minutes or hours later looking as though a storm had passed through. But I sing as I tidy up the place. He did that for me and Tom. He put a song in our hearts and a smile on our faces. I don't wear his image on a bracelet or necklace as some grandmothers do. I don't need a set in a ring to represent his birthday. I wear my love for him, and his for me, deep in my heart.

When life gets cloudy, I remember something funny he said, or in my mind I see him standing at the fair—small, windblown, dirty, a bundle of excitement—and my soul breathes a sigh of contentment. Yes, I'm proud to be a member in good standing of the Silly Old Grandmas Club. You probably belong too if you have a grandchild.

A WONDERFUL JOB
by Johnnie

I didn't want grandchildren. My busy schedule would not allow me any time to spend with them, so when my daughter Elaine announced, after five years of marriage, that this blessed event would soon be . . . I exclaimed disgustedly, "I hope it's a girl then."

He came just before Christmas. We gazed at him with pride through the hospital nursery window. But when we had our first physical contact with him, he grabbed my finger and I know he smiled at me. I was hooked and I have always had plenty of time for him. I wouldn't trade him for a thousand old girls.

Five years later, our Sara Lain came. This time I couldn't wait for our baby's appearance. She looks like her other grandmother, but is a "doer" like me. Our house will never be the same. She visits often and always leaves it looking like the city dump. She takes our dining-room chairs, along with some old sheets, to make a tent in the middle of our living-room floor. When she becomes bored with this, she moves to her next messy project. She gets out her acrylic paints and proceeds to paint pictures. She can finish a painting in less than an hour. That done, she decides to sew. Sara can cut out a doll dress without a pattern and sew it up. My sewing machine is smoking when she is through.

She keeps moving on to her next project without ever cleaning up after herself. She leaves my house looking as though some supernatural power picked it up, shook it, and allowed its contents to stay where they fell. Without complaining, we clean up again and thank God for this happy, talented little girl.

She wants to be just like Granny when she grows up.

Grandmawing is the most rewarding and the best job I've ever had.

THE OLD MAN AND THE BOY
by Johnnie

It warms my heart to see
The gray-haired old man and the young boy
Happy together and as busy as a bee.
Twelve years ago when the boy was three
His "Daggie" was young and stronger than he.
They were an inseparable pair, the man and the boy,
And as the years flew by they brought each other great joy.
Daggie took him fishing and to baseball games;
Dagg's voice would soften when he spoke the boy's name.
Time quickly passed; big buddies they stayed.
The old man and the boy, their places did trade.
Now the boy is strong, nearly six feet tall;
The old man is frail, but his life is a ball.
Mark takes *him* fishing and to baseball games,
And Mark's voice softens when he speaks Daggie's name.

LIFE'S CHANGING SEASONS
by Johnnie

Most warm summer days you'll find me sitting on our patio gazing at the last mad stir of blooms from our rose garden. As my grandson Markie and I sit here this day, several flowers on each bush are bursting with magnificent colors of red, pink, melon, white, and yellow. There's even one light-blue flower. A hummingbird gathers nectar from one, then another. His tiny wings move so quickly, he appears motionless.

Markie has never seen a hummingbird. He watches, still and quiet, an unusual pose for Markie. I watch him now, rather than nature's beauty, and I think, What a miracle he is. Without him many of the wonders of another changing season would pass me by completely. I silently say, Thank you, God, for giving him to us.

The little bird finishes feeding and flies away. Markie immediately notices a red squirrel sitting at the end of our driveway. He whispers, "Look, Granny. That squirrel stole one of our pecans. He better be careful or a car'll get 'im when he crosses the street." For a brief moment the little squirrel sits there on his hind legs, his front paws holding the pecan. He really does appear to be looking both ways, anticipating crossing the street. Soon he senses our presence and scampers away.

Markie's mother comes for him, and I'm left alone with my thoughts. Many seasons have changed for me, but with a child around, I'm seeing them anew again.

Life has its seasons. Markie is our breath of spring, our new beginning; his parents, our summer, the season of growth. Tom and I are the fall season. We, like the trees in fall, are losing our sap. Mama is our example of winter. She sits quietly, her hair white and shiny like the new-fallen snow, a feature that softens her wise face and puts a bright sparkle in her eyes.

Sometimes I feel that life is passing me by, though as I look back I wouldn't want to change the wonderful life I've experienced. I expect to be in heaven after the winter season of my life; however, I prefer to stay here as long as possible, surrounded by loved ones, enjoying the changing seasons.

HOW HIGH IS UP?

by Johnnie

I kept my five-year-old grandson for his mother while she delivered his baby sister. I learned a lot. "Gran, how high is up? Does God ever sleep? If reindeer can fly, why can't horses? When I grow up will you still be old?"

I tried to answer as best I could. "Well, Mark, up is as high as you can see, then add as far as from your house to Gran's. God catches a nap between tendin' to all our needs. Santa's reindeer can fly because he sprinkles them with magic dust. Horses could fly too if only we had some magic dust."

I ignored the age question, hoping he would forget he asked. I tried hard to answer every other question. I can't say whether I was especially attentive because he missed his mother so much, or because I wanted to stay on that pedestal where he placed me. Maybe it was a little of both.

Like all grannies, I do so enjoy his unselfish and total love. He is the only person I know who loves me exactly the way I am. He wouldn't change anything about me, even if he could. I wonder how many more years he will believe that Granny knows all there is to know.

THE WAY TO A MOTHER-IN-LAW'S HEART
by Ibbie

We were very pleased when our son married the lovely girl he had been dating for two years. They lived in a city 150 miles away and came to visit once a month. Having heard so many stories about conflict between mother- and daughter-in-law, I did not intend for that to happen to us, so I was careful not to pry or interfere in their life and Sharron and I became good friends.

They had been married two years when our first grandchild was born. Of course, I wanted to spoil him and smother him with love, but again I was careful not to interfere.

Their visit, on a beautiful summer weekend when Stevie was two years old, had been a joyful time. He was allowed to play in the creek near our house and do anything his little heart desired. Having enjoyed the creek so much, Stevie began begging to go back again just before going home. Sharron had just bathed and dressed him in a cute shorts outfit and white tennis shoes and socks. She said, "You know you can't wade in the creek with your shoes on, don't you?" "Please let Granny take me," he begged. "I'll just throw rocks in the water and you won't let me get dirty, will you, Granny?"

"I'll *carry* him," I promised. Sharron gave us permission and away we went, Stevie and I, leaving the others behind to pack the car for their trip home.

I started out carrying the little angel in my arms but he soon wanted to walk. Thinking I could watch closely and not let him get dirty, I put him down, not noticing the mud-hole a few feet away. Well, right through the puddle he went, soaking his shoes and socks with muddy water; some even splashed on his shorts. What was I to do? I really dreaded facing Sharron, not knowing how she would react. If she was angry I hoped she would take it out on me. I didn't think I could bear it if she spanked Stevie. I said, "We must tell

Mom we're sorry your clean clothes are ruined."

As we approached the house, Sharron, Steve, and Granddaddy were outside waiting for us. Stevie ran to Sharron and exclaimed, "Mom, Granny and I are sorry as can be but I got my clothes wet and dirty!" Sharron smiled sweetly and said, "Well, as long as you're sorry I guess it's okay. Let's go change."

I let out a big sigh of relief, and at that moment I fell in love with my daughter-in-law—forever! The next year they blessed us with another "grand" son named Tray. All barriers are down now and we are a close family. I know I can spoil them and love them without reservation. Aren't I a lucky mother-in-law and granny?

A BOX FROM THE HEART
by Ibbie

Our four-year-old granddaughter Deidra lived 350 miles away, and only came to visit twice a year. She was at that inquisitive age, wanting to explore every drawer, closet, and cabinet, and I allowed it, explaining that it was okay at Granny's house, but not anywhere else.

She slept in my prettiest silk nightgown and wore my dresses and high-heeled shoes. She was allowed to paint her fingernails (and mine!), to use lotions and powder, and to explore my jewelry box—even to wear some of the jewelry. She was having the time of her life.

Having gone through every drawer in the bureau except the top one, which she couldn't reach, she asked, "What's in that drawer, Granny?!"

"That's my keepsake drawer, Deidra."

"What's a keepsake drawer, Granny?"

"That's where I keep all the things people give me that are very special."

"I want ta see, Granny! Hold me up so I can see!" she cried, jumping with excitement. I pulled up a chair for her to stand on before the opened drawer. The first thing she spied was *the box*.

It was a red heart-shaped box with a beautiful corsage of red roses and baby's breath covering the top. The trim around the edge was lace with a red ribbon running through it. A big red bow topped it all off. The flowers and ribbon were faded, but that just seemed to make the box more intriguing for Deidra. She gasped as she lifted it out of the drawer, exclaiming, "Oh, Granny, it's so pretty! Can I have it?!" Memories of the box came flooding back as Deidra persisted, "Can I have it, Granny?! Can I?!"

I sighed and said, "Some day, Deidra. Maybe for your birthday." Then I told her the story of the box.

"Granddaddy gave me this box filled with candy on our

first Valentine's Day together. All I really expected was a Valentine card, for we'd only been married a month and didn't have much money. Granddaddy couldn't afford a fancy box of candy, but he bought it anyway, spending a large portion of his paycheck. That candy had to serve as part of our food for that week."

"Can I have it, Granny?!"

Debby said, "Mother, you shouldn't give her that box. It means so much to you, and she'll just tear it up."

"I won't neider, Mother. And Granny really wants me to have it. Don't you, Granny?" Deidra asked, with a pout on her sweet face.

"Wait until your birthday and we'll see," I said. I allowed Deidra to play carefully with the box every day during her visit, returning it to the keepsake drawer at night. Although it seemed kind of foolish holding on to a faded old box when it gave a little girl so much pleasure, I was not quite ready to part with it.

In the three months that followed, I took the box out of the drawer several times. Each time Deidra's sweet, excited face would flash before my eyes, so I had to include it in the package I gave her for her fifth birthday. Debby said it was the most treasured gift Deidra received, but again warned me it would probably be torn up during her play.

Now, as Deidra grows into her teens, I wonder if I should have waited and given the box when she could grasp its real meaning. I feel sure it no longer exists, and hesitate to ask for fear she won't remember. I'd rather recall her lovingly taking it out of the drawer each day that summer so long ago, her young eyes sparkling with wonder and excitement as she asked, "Can I have it, Granny?! Can I?!"

LOVE IS RISKY
by Johnnie

I thought *Love Story,* the movie, was better on TV than in the movie theater. Why? Most of the bad language was bleeped out. The plot was beautiful, and it started me thinking about the day in February set aside each year for sweethearts to remember that special one in their lives.

I began to wonder what love really is. The dictionary gives many meanings for love. The one I like best reads, "A profoundly tender affection for another person." It appears to me, then, that there should never be just one day set aside to show love. It should be an everyday thing.

There are so many different kinds of love, the word can seem overwhelming. In *Love Story* they defined love as "never having to say you're sorry." I disagree. Some of the sweetest times for two people who love each other are when they patch up a misunderstanding with the words I'm sorry. Those two words bring such joy and relief to both parties.

The rich father and son in the movie never understood each other. It was always evident that the "tender affection" was there, but neither one would give an inch to let the other know. Love must be given away, or it is worthless. We sometimes hesitate to give our love away because we fear rejection and hurt. Even when this happens, we are stronger for having given. Remember the cuddly kitten or puppy you loved so much as a child, and how badly it hurt when your pet died? But you learned so many things about life and caring for others from that experience.

You can't see love; you can't hear it, touch it, smell it, or taste it; but you can feel it. God in His wisdom planned our lives all the way through from birth to the grave around that very special emotion, love. First He gave us parents, then spouse, next children; and for our twilight years, He gave us the sweetest love of all—*grandchildren.*

Chapter 2

About Parents

MEMORIES

by Ibbie

Whenever I close my eyes
I can see
A farmhouse filled with love and
Comfort for me,
And a very large yard with many oak trees.
Mama and Papa had ten children in all;
They watched over and loved us from the time
We were small
To when we grew up and stood straight and tall.
They taught us, too,
That life could be tough,
But to call on God
When the going got rough.

THE BIOSPHERE
by Ibbie

They should have asked Papa how to feed eight people on 3.15 acres:

On September 27, 1993, Biosphere 2's crew of four men and four women emerged from the 3.15-acre dome. Biosphere 2 was funded by private donations at a cost of $150 million. If Papa were alive, they could have saved all that money by asking him how he fed twelve people on a few acres of Tennessee farmland.

First off, he would never have chosen a desert in which to try to raise food. Secondly, the Biosphere crew was definitely wearing the wrong kind of clothes. You can't work in the dirt wearing fancy outfits that make you look like aliens from outer space. You have to use common sense about such things. What they needed were overalls and plow shoes.

Actually, Papa owned eighty acres, but I think he could have made it on 3.15 acres. He worked the land with two mules and a pretty, spotted pony. The pony was used for plowing the garden and other patches, and for riding. The mules did the heavy work. We had chickens and hogs to produce our eggs and meat, and cows to give us milk and butter. Besides the acre of garden where a variety of vegetables was grown, there was a tomato patch, a pea patch, a watermelon and cantaloupe patch, a strawberry patch, and an orchard with apple, peach, pear, and cherry trees. Enough corn was planted to supply us and the animals. The remainder of the land was planted in cotton, the "cash" crop. Money from the cotton bought flour, coffee, and sugar—about all that was needed to supplement our diet.

We always had clean, fresh air. No oxygen needed to be pumped in for us. During the spring the scent of honeysuckle and sweet williams filled the air, along with the aroma of fried chicken from the kitchen. Winter led to the smell of wood smoke, a smell so common back then I hardly noticed, but now every time I get a whiff of wood smoke it brings back pleasant memories of family gathered around the fireplace.

The Bio crew had to open up once to get more seed. Every good farmer knows you should save seed every year for the next planting. The dome was also opened to supply the crew with sleeping pills, mousetraps, and makeup. After we worked all day on the farm, sleep was not a problem for us. Cats took care of the mice, and all the makeup we had was poke berries to color our lips.

In contrast to the Bio men and women, Mama and Papa were never asked if they had sex. That was obvious, for they had ten children. Large families were common in those days, but the topic of sex was never mentioned in mixed company, and any man or woman suspected of having an affair outside marriage was chastised severely by society.

The Biosphere was just an experiment, but I think it proved how difficult it is for people today to get along *without* the modern conveniences of everyday life and *with* the immorality so prevalent in our culture. Whether it's 3.15 acres in a dome, or eighty fertile acres in Tennessee, you need old-fashioned ideas to get the job done in an old-fashioned way. Those Biosphere people should have just talked to an old fella in overalls.

A LITTLE GIRL'S DAY
by Ibbie

I slipped out of bed before anyone else with thoughts of surprising Mama on Mother's Day: I was going to cook breakfast for the whole family! Though I was only ten years old, I had helped Mama many times in the kitchen and felt sure that I could manage all by myself.

The skillet I needed was hanging on the wall behind the stove. A can in which Mama stored fried meat grease was sitting on the stove right under that skillet. With the help of a kitchen chair, I reached up and unhooked the skillet. Being iron, the skillet was much heavier than I thought, and down it fell—knocking the grease can to the floor. Grease splattered all over the stove, cabinets, and most of the floor. What a mess!

When Mama entered the kitchen a while later, I was down on my hands and knees trying to clean up with a towel. The grease on the floor caused it to shine as if it had been waxed. Mama exclaimed, "Oh! You're so smart! You've scrubbed and waxed the floor!" I burst into tears, and between sobs told my pitiful story. Mama gathered me in her arms and said, "It's all right, honey. If the grease hadn't spilled I'm sure you could have made a fine breakfast. You can still cook; I'll help you just like you often help me. Tell me what to do and we'll get started.

"But first, wouldn't you say it'll take some hot soapy water to get this grease up?"

"Yes, Mama. I'll get a bucket and mop."

"Now that the floor's clean, what are you going to make for breakfast?"

"Let's make flap jacks, Mama!"

"Whatever you say, honey. It's your treat."

I retrieved the mixing bowl from the cabinet and measured the flour while Mama broke the eggs and added milk. I stirred the mix while Mama rubbed the skillet with butter and placed it on the stove.

"This batter's so smooth. I'll wager it's gonna make delicious flap jacks," Mama said as she spooned some into the hot skillet.

"Let me turn it, Mama," I said. She handed the turner over to me, holding me so I wouldn't fall onto the stove.

The first two or three flap jacks didn't turn out very well. I'm sure Mama's thoughts were to remind me of an easier chore for a ten-year-old when she said, "Are we going to eat in the kitchen or the dining room?"

"Let's eat in the dining room and use the good dishes! I'll set the table!" I cried excitedly as I jumped down from the chair, leaving the making of the flap jacks to Mama. She proceeded to prepare a delicious breakfast, all the time asking my advice and making me feel as if I were in charge and doing it all by myself. When everything was ready, Mama remarked what a treat it was having someone cook breakfast for her on Mother's Day. Mama made me very happy that day, turning Mother's Day into Little Girl's Day. But then, she could always make everything right in my world.

Mothers are so special. Let's remember to honor them every day, not just one day a year.

THANKS, MOM!
by Ibbie

Betty was so annoyed with her daughter-in-law Debby. Two babies in four years of marriage—and pregnant again—it was just too much! How would Debby and Steve ever feed and clothe three children on Steve's salary? Why hadn't Debby taken her birth control pills? My eighty-year-old neighbor Mrs. Murry laughingly said, "If I'd had birth control pills when I was young, I would have taken 'em by the handful."

I couldn't help but wonder which of Mrs. Murry's five children she would have chosen not to have. Would it have been the son she made her home with as she grew old and wasn't able to live alone? How about the son who drove fifty miles every week to visit her and bring her gifts? Would it have been the son who owned a clothing store and saw that she had nice clothes to wear at no cost to her? Or maybe the daughter who stayed with her day and night while she was in the hospital? Or perhaps it would have been the boy, named after Mrs. Murry's husband, who had lived to be only seven years old and whom Mrs. Murry often remembered with tears.

Having been born into a large family, I often think about how many of us might never have been born if birth control pills had been available back then. Would my older sister Margaret, who took care of Mama during the last years of her life, have been born? It's really kind of scary to think about!

GOOD SWAP
by Ibbie

Mama, in her nineties and almost blind, had become very distrustful of people, especially where money was concerned. She could see only shadows, but was very alert to what was happening around her. At a family gathering, my sister Margaret told this story of a trip to the bank with Mama.

As they drove up to the bank window, Mama handed Margaret a $50 check that she wanted to cash. Meanwhile, Margaret proceeded to fill out a check of her own for $25. Mama said, with suspicion in her voice, "What're you doing writing on my check?"

"I'm not writing on your check. I'm writing one that I want cashed."

"How much is your check for?!" Mama asked.

"It's for $25."

"Well, tell them to put mine in a separate envelope!"

Margaret, being the good daughter that she is, gave the teller Mama's instructions. When the transaction was complete, Margaret handed Mama her envelope and stuck the other one in her purse. As they drove along Mama kept feeling the bills and holding them up to the light. Margaret was trying to ignore her, and was wondering if Mama thought the bank had given her counterfeit bills, when Mama said in a "um hum, I got you!" voice, "Margaret! You gave me the wrong envelope!"

"I don't think so, Mama," Margaret said, "but we'll check." Margaret pulled over to the curb, took the envelope out of her purse and explained, "You have the right one. See?" She held up the bills. "My envelope has two ten-dollar bills and a five. Yours has two twenties and a ten. Okay?"

They had been driving along quietly for awhile, Mama still fingering the bills, when she said, "I think you're wrong, but I guess I'll have to take your word for it!"

After Margaret finished telling the story, my brother-in-law Tom piped up and said, "Hey, Marg, why didn't you just swap with her?"

Margaret exclaimed, "Yeah, why didn't I think of that?"

JUST BEHAVE
by Ibbie

Mama tried to instill in her children the importance of behaving. We were to behave ourselves when playing together, especially in the house. No wrestling or running was allowed. We had to behave at the dinner table, in school and church, in our marriages, and anytime we were out in public.

My brother and his wife divorced. A few years later they worked out their problems and remarried. Mama said, "Now, you all behave yourselves and get on with your lives."

In *Webster's Dictionary*, the definition of the word behave is "to conduct or comport oneself." They should have added "in a way that would make your mother proud." The world would be a better place if everyone would heed Mama's advice and simply behave themselves.

HOME
by Johnnie

I think the word "home" is one of the sweetest, warmest, most beautiful words in the English language. When I see or hear the word "home," my mind travels with joy to my childhood.

I remember a big two-story farmhouse, heated in winter by fireplaces in every room and cooled in summer by high ceilings with lots of windows and huge oak trees. I remember the large dining-room table, piled high with golden fried chicken. Many a Sunday, a freezer of homemade ice cream took its place at the table, too.

Not only did Mama, Papa, and ten children occupy our home, but there were often extras. We knew Mama would never fail to make our friends feel welcome. She'd even stir up a cake or fry potatoes for special treats.

We were poor money-wise, but we kids never knew. Most families in our area lived within the same means as we, so there was no comparison to make between rich and poor.

An unwritten law in our home was "everybody works"! But Papa made work fun. He always bragged about how much cotton we picked or how well I could gather the down row of corn. When quitting time arrived, we would head home to the wonderful aroma of corn bread in the oven, white beans in the iron pot, stewed potatoes, and often a platter of country ham and red-eye gravy. A pile of biscuits would round out a great meal. After supper, we'd all gather round the radio to hear "Lum and Abner," our evening entertainment.

The old farmhouse no longer exists. Mama and Papa are gone. The ten brothers and sisters have dwindled to six, scattered from Michigan to Tennessee. The memories, however, linger on.

We all have our own homes now. The nostalgia and

traditions of the old days have disappeared in most cases, but home is still home. No matter where we go in life, home is that special place to which we all want to return.

PAPA

by Johnnie

The gravestone read, February 4, 1889 - April 23, 1961. The small stone beside it read, December 15, 1931 - August 24, 1932. As I stood alone in the old country cemetery by Papa's grave, memories of him flooded my heart. I didn't bring flowers because he was always allergic to them. But with Father's Day drawing nigh, it was fitting to visit and remember Papa.

To write "Papa was" instead of "Papa is" brings a lump the size of a grapefruit to my throat. Papa was short and plump and part Irishman, a super guy whose sense of humor was catchy. His word was his bond. His kids were his life. Papa never spanked, and he rarely scolded. He didn't have to. We all tried hard to please him simply because he was so good to us. He used to play dominoes with us, and would always turn the double blank backwards in his hand. We thought he was so dumb then. But as I stand here now, I can hear the snickers of glee this act always brought from the other small players. He knew what he was doing.

The gravestone beside Papa's brings back some of my very first memories of him, and of the day his young son Tom died. I was four years old then. We lived in our two-story farmhouse, miles from the nearest neighbor. Not only were the rooms huge in our home, but the ceilings were twelve feet tall. To a four-year-old each room looked very large indeed.

The day Tom died, Mama had put him to sleep on a double bed instead of his baby bed, pushing the double bed against the wall on one side and stacking pillows around Tom on the other three sides. I've often wondered why she did that, but I could never bring myself to ask her.

Mama told me to stay with Tom while she picked vegetables from her garden.

She knew I was scared to be alone in that big house, and

when I called her saying that the baby had fallen off the bed, she thought I was crying wolf, and kept gathering food. When she finally did come back in, she found the baby hung between the bed and the wall. She grabbed him and ran, crying hysterically, to Papa, who was plowing the fields a half-mile away. I was so frightened; I cried uncontrollably. I tried to follow but couldn't keep up. In Mama's shock and grief she had forgotten all about me. Halfway to Papa, stumbling over fresh-plowed earth, I fell to the ground, exhausted.

I remember Papa trying to revive Tom. When he quickly saw it was no use, he handed the baby back to Mama, then spied me all dirty and crying. He picked me up and gently carried me home, assuring me all the way, "It's not your fault."

I was too little to be fully aware of the earthshaking drama that had just transpired. Papa was sad. I was afraid. Then one day, Papa gathered all his family around him and said, "It's time to bury the guilt. Our living children need us. Let's all stop looking back." True to his words, from that day forward he once again became our fun-loving Papa.

I smile as I remember him walking across the barnyard one afternoon, when suddenly one of the boys opened a gate which held a raging, stomping, fifteen-hundred-pound bull. The animal snorted, looked Papa's way, and headed toward him at breakneck speed. Papa heard the commotion, peered over his shoulder, and with no trouble cleared the tall fence that was six steps away in one full leap just as the bull charged into it. Everybody, including Papa, laughed.

The older boys played many tricks on Papa, sometimes dangerous ones, but he never got mad. One time Top gave Papa a shot of cholera medicine which had been prepared for one of the animals. It only made him a little sick, but it could have killed him.

I became Papa's sidekick during World War II, when

there were no able-bodied men left at home to work the farm. Papa had asthma so severe that he couldn't ride the tractor, so I took over the job. Manual labor was not something women did back in those days, but times were changing. I was sixteen, and enjoyed doing something different.

Papa's asthma became emphysema, and he literally couldn't breathe at times. Remembering Papa's last years brings to mind a story I once heard. I don't remember the source, let alone the author, but the story goes something like this: three teenage boys were waiting for a traffic light to change from red to green. They were joking, laughing, shoving one another, like kids do, when they saw a stooped old man standing alone waiting at the light. Two of the boys made fun of the old man's sagging shoulders, wrinkled skin, balding head, and labored breathing. The third boy paused beside the old man and whispered, "I'll help you across, if you wish to go." Gratefully, the old man placed his gnarled hand on the strong young arm. The young man guided the old man's trembling feet along, glad that his own were firm and strong. The other boys teased, but our hero said, "He's some boy's father, you know, no matter that he's grown old and slow." And that night, somebody's father bowed his head at home, praying, "God, be kind to that noble boy, who is somebody's pride and joy."

Papa taught not by word but by deed. He taught us to work, to be honest, and to stand up for what we believe in; but most of all, he taught us that life is precious and can be a ball, all the way through. Thank God for fathers like him. If your dad is living, tell him how much he means to you, before it's too late.

I BELIEVE IN YOU
by Johnnie

I recently watched a country music awards show on TV and was shocked to see one of the performers come on stage wearing faded, patched jeans and a flannel shirt with some of the buttons missing. The cuffs of the shirt were turned up once and flapped as he walked. An old hat—battered, dirty, and worn—adorned his head. His shoes looked as if they had died a slow, agonizing death.

I didn't quite catch his name . . . it was odd, Hobo somebody or Dining Car Dave, or some kind of silly name like that.

Another shock came when he stepped to the microphone and began to sing "I Believe in You." His voice was so clear and the words so sweet that I forgot what he looked like and was lost, almost in a trance, as he sang. I really didn't care anymore what he looked like. I thought, This is the way mothers feel about their children.

We may look tacky on the outside and be ornery on the inside, but Mom will still say, "I believe in you."

Let's talk about one such mom. Maybe this describes your mother. Like the song says, she believed in babies. She brought up a large family during the Great Depression. Late at night after everybody else was in bed, this mother could be found at her sewing machine, making dresses for her girls and shirts for her boys from printed feed sacks. The clothes always looked store-bought when she finished.

She cooked three meals every day from scratch on a wood-burning stove. She even cut the wood herself, with an ax, because her husband and sons worked from daylight till dark in the fields. Her garden was the best in the area, providing enough food to see her family through the winter. Canning six hundred quarts of food a year was her minimum goal.

She believed in love, too. She would gather her brood

around her and sing or read aloud. She was shy about saying I love you often, but her actions always let her children know that they were loved.

Financially, things got better for her family after the depression. Some of her children even earned high school diplomas—something she was always proud of, since she had only finished the sixth grade.

This mother saved egg and milk money for several weeks to buy a special graduation dress for one of her daughters. She didn't know that the dress was supposed to be white, so she surprised her daughter with a pink dress, because pink was her daughter's favorite color. The mother still grieves, a half-century later, because her child was different on that all-important night.

The years have passed slowly. The mother is ninety-plus now. Her eyesight is dim; she can only see the shapes of objects. Her hearing is almost gone. She walks with a turtle-slow shuffle. She says, "I'm so tired, I wish the Lord would take me home and get me out of my children's way."

"But Mom," I say, "who then would tell me, 'I believe in you?' And Mom, I always loved that pink dress."

ME AND MAMA AND SHIRLEY TEMPLE
by Johnnie

Mama never received, asked for, or even expected many opportunities to do her own thing. She did have one strong desire, however, that *almost* came true. She desperately wanted to see a Shirley Temple movie.

She had heard about Shirley on our battery-operated radio, and could scarcely believe such a little girl could perform as well as people said she did. Mama talked about how wonderful it would be to go to the theater in town and see a Shirley Temple movie, never dreaming that she would actually get to go; after all, only twice in her entire life had she even been to a movie theater.

One day Papa came home from town and said to Mama, "Ms. Eva, there's a Shirley Temple movie showing in town. You and me's going to town and you're gonna see you a Shirley Temple show. We're leaving the younguns at home. I'm not going in myself. No use wasting money on a ticket for me since I don't care much about a picture show. I'll wait for you on the courthouse bench."

Mama was so excited, but then she made her first big mistake. She said, "George, Johnnie should go, too. She's the same age as Shirley [Shirley and I were four then] and I think she'll enjoy the movie. It won't cost anything for Johnnie to get in." Mama scoffed at Papa's objections, so it was decided I could go.

I was so excited! I had never seen a movie. However, the movie was not to be the highlight of my evening. The wondrous things in the movie *theater,* things I'd never seen before, were what interested me the most.

We left home about an hour before showtime in Papa's old Model T Ford truck, allowing plenty of time to drive the ten miles to town. Papa said he wanted to get there early so Ms. Eva wouldn't miss a single minute of the show. When we arrived, poor Mama made her second big mistake. She decided we had plenty of time before the movie started to take me to the bathroom.

I never knew there could be a toilet indoors, and had never seen one flush. I was so fascinated, I forgot about the movie, opting to stay in the bathroom. I wondered why Mama objected. Why would anyone rather watch a little girl dance than see the wonder that happened every time I pulled the chain? The water made a swishing noise, the soft paper disappeared, then the crazy thing filled itself back up with water. Every time! Where in the world did that water come from, and where did it go? The paper that rolled right off when I pulled sure was soft, much softer than the Sears catalog we used back home.

Mama finally dragged me into the dark movie theater, with me protesting loudly all the way. After Papa's efforts to get Mama there on time, she still missed the beginning of the movie. I sat quietly for awhile, but I could not get my mind off the wonder of the toilet. I didn't much like sitting in the dark, either, so I whispered, "Mama, I have to be excused."

"Not now, hon. Watch Shirley Temple dance."

"I have to go, Mama. I'll just go by myself," I said as I darted past her into the aisle and back to that marvelous room.

Back inside the bathroom, I noticed another chain hanging from the ceiling that I hadn't seen before. I wondered what would happen if I pulled it. I jumped as high as I could, barely able to grab the chain for a jerk, just as Mama stepped in the door and yelled, "No!" It was too late! The room became pitch dark and scared me nearly to death. I screamed, "Mama!" over and over at the top of my lungs. She was right behind me, but let me stew awhile before she reached out to me. Since she was so exasperated, I don't think she really cared that I was frightened, and since she didn't know what made the light go out or how to turn it back on, I think she was a little frightened herself.

An usher heard my cry and came to our rescue. Still trembling, we went back into the theater. The movie was almost over, and Mama hadn't even seen half of it.

During her golden years, Mama moved to town and had all the modern conveniences: electricity, TV, even a bathroom. She often got to watch Shirley Temple on TV, but to her dying day Mama would still grumble, good-humoredly, about *almost* seeing a Shirley Temple movie.

PLEASE PASS THE SYRUP
by Johnnie

That high-brow Polaner All Fruit commercial on TV (where they make fun of the man who says "please pass the jelly" instead of calling the product "All Fruit") brought back a fond memory to my sister Margaret. She harked back to the time when we lived in a big two-story farmhouse with high ceilings and great big rooms. The dining room was twenty feet long, and Papa had made a table to fit it.

That table seated lots of people for a meal. Once, for about a three-week period, Mama fed several working men at that table. One of those men was Mr. Burson, an educated city fella who bought a stand of chestnut timber from Mr. Charlie Price, our landlord. Mr. Burson hired several local men to cut the timber by hand and snake it out of the woods with mules, paying them the unheard-of wage of $1.25 a day. He also hired Mama to cook dinner (the noontime meal) for the whole bunch.

Mama gathered us kids around her and said, "Now kids, Mr. Burson is a fine, educated man. We want him to think well of us. When we eat today, try to show him that you have some table manners." Then Mama removed the everyday oilcloth tablecloth, replacing it with a crisply starched white cotton one.

Paper napkins and paper towels weren't to be found among farm folk back in those days, so Mama placed a white cloth napkin by each plate—which was also pretty uncommon. The feast she prepared, however, was something we were used to: vegetables, fried chicken, country ham, banana pudding—the works.

The loggers came in, washed up, and sat down at the table. Mama set up a table on the side for us kids. Wallace, age five, looked at the big table and said in a loud voice, "Mama, I wish you'd use this rag tablecloth all the time! Don't never put that ol' leather'n back on!" He picked up one of the napkins and said, "What's this?! We ain't never had these before!" Then he got up and reached over Mr. Burson to get the bowl of mashed sweet potatoes covered with marshmallows, and proceeded to rake the whole marshmallow top onto his plate, talking loudly all the while about how Mama had never put marshmallows on the potatoes before. Wallace finally settled down to eat, and the men began to fill their plates.

The locals felt kind of like Wallace did. They didn't know what to do with those cloth napkins, either. Mr. Burson was obviously amused with the whole thing, but was very complimentary to Mama about all that delicious-looking food, and was not shy about filling his plate high with her fine vittles. But before digging in, he looked around the table and said, "One more thing and I'm ready to eat. Sam, will you please pass the syrup?"

Sam, a grown cousin of ours, answered, "Huh?" His eyes searched frantically all around the table as Mama walked in from the kitchen and pointed to the jar of sorghum molasses sitting at Sam's elbow. Sam, a bit embarrassed, but trying to be nonchalant about it, sheepishly grabbed the molasses jar and said, "Aw, here's the 'lasses."

As Margaret put it, "Mama pert neer passed out."

GRADUATION: A TIME TO LOOSEN THE TIES
by Johnnie

High school graduation in these troubled times is a mixture of joy and sadness for parents. We know we must let go, but we'd like to hold on. This is the story of what one father I know felt on graduation night. He says, "The speaker's voice had a steady rise and fall, and I didn't hear what he was saying. I was looking through the crowd at the back of my son's head, overwhelmed with emotion. Recalling the last eighteen years of my son's life kept my mind occupied.

"I remembered the elation when I saw the doctor's face appear in the waiting-room door and he said, 'You have a healthy eight-pound boy.' I wanted to climb to the top of the Empire State Building and shout, 'I have a son! I have a son!'

"I thought back to the first time I took him fishing. He was only four years old then, and when he pulled his first fish from the water there was such a look of awe on his face that I couldn't help but hug him tightly. He danced around excitedly and yelled, 'Daddy, hurry, let's get the hook back in the water and catch another one!'

"I was so caught up in remembering times with my son, I forgot where I was and laughed out loud. My wife poked me, reminding me where I was. Then I began thinking of my son's first day of school. He was so little, and so fearful of the unknown. How I had wanted to go with him! To hold his hand and to be there the whole day, letting my presence comfort him.

"But just as I had to let him go alone on that long-ago day, so it was that I had to do so once again. In my heart I knew it was the right thing to do, but it hurt so much."

THE SUPREME SACRIFICE
by Johnnie

"Regret to inform you—stop—your son, Wallace, missing-in-action—stop—presumed dead—stop."

The Western Union operator didn't relay the dreaded telegram to our home immediately. It had arrived at one in the morning, and the operator didn't see the use of disturbing Mama and Papa. She had known our family all her life, and she knew that plenty of sleepless nights lay ahead. Instead, she called Mrs. Barnett, our neighbor, to ask her to be there in the morning when she broke the news.

It was 1944. The war was almost over. Wallace, nineteen years old, was killed during the last day of fighting in the Paulau Islands. Like the telegram repeated over and over, our home life did *stop*. It's hard to describe the pain, so different from a death where the family members are able to bury the body. There is such a helpless feeling.

Papa walked the floor day and night. He said he had heard the Barnetts' phone ring late the night before we got the news, and had thought that they must be receiving bad news of some kind. (Telephones were party-line phones then. There were eight people on the same line, and everyone could hear everyone else's ring.) Papa said that a very lonely feeling had come over him. He thought about Wallace, breathed a silent prayer for his safety, and then turned over and went back to sleep.

Mama sat like a zombie, saying nothing. Both she and Papa were angry and frustrated. They were proud of their Marine son. He gave his life willingly, they knew, but the agony of losing him was almost unbearable. Days passed before they could even talk about it.

The rest of the family kept things going as usual. I was seventeen at the time. Wallace and I were close in age, and we had been big buddies. We had played together, gotten into mischief together—we had even earned whippings together, because neither would tell on the other. But it all seemed so unreal to me. He had been gone for a whole year, and at that age, a year is like an eternity. I couldn't believe he had really died.

Life went on. The Purple Heart came. Mama couldn't even look at it; Papa pretended we never received it. They were aware of its significance, but to them the Purple Heart in the beautiful box represented their son's life, and it hurt too much to even look upon it.

In 1948 the government gave us the choice of bringing his body home or leaving it overseas. Papa wanted to bring him home. He said we would bury him in Memphis in the National Cemetery.

The graveside service was set for 11:00 A.M., but at the last minute Papa couldn't bring himself to go. Mama took her cue from him and stayed behind too. As the rest of us left, I saw Papa sitting in a straight chair leaning forward, his head on his arms against the porch rail. His hair was white and thinning on top. He was sobbing from the depths of his soul. Mama, strong and dry-eyed, stood behind him, a firm hand on his shoulder. It was a picture we never forgot.

To me, the playing of "Taps" is the loneliest sound on earth. Next was the ear-shattering twenty-one-gun salute. During the salute my oldest brother cried out, "Why couldn't *You* have taken me instead, Lord?"

Thousands of families like ours experienced the pain we went through. The hurt never goes away; it just dulls. Mama still has the flag that draped his casket. She can look at the Purple Heart now. His picture hangs on the wall, the memory of him so special to her, and to us all. But the pain is still apparent in her eyes when she speaks of him.

Everyone was inconvenienced terribly during the war, but not all made the supreme sacrifice. If not for the thousands upon thousands of boys who gave their lives in World War II, we all would likely be slaves now. When I stand gazing at the rows and rows of gravestones in the Memphis cemetery, and think of the thousands of cemeteries that contain our heroic men, tears well in my eyes, thankfulness penetrates my heart, and I'm humbled. I hear in my mind the clear, booming voice of Kate Smith as she sings "God Bless America, My Home Sweet Home."

Chapter 3

Love and Marriage

THE TEST OF TIME
by Ibbie

"Good day to you, Dear Valentine," read the inscription on the card everyone was given as we entered our club meeting. Valentine's Day was near and we were to begin with this line and add lyrics to create a card for someone. The cards would be judged at the end of the meeting. I addressed mine to my husband of more than forty years:

"Good day to you, Dear Valentine.
I know you'll always be mine;
For our love has stood the test of time."

Mine won!

TILL DEATH DO US PART
by Johnnie

A large section in the Sunday paper usually features weddings. It mainly has articles on how to have the perfect wedding. But often when a couple is planning their perfect wedding, they don't seem to want the marriage that must follow to get in the way.

What is a perfect wedding? I went to a wedding once where the flower girl was so nervous she got sick and threw up all over the stage. Perfect wedding ruined.

Another wedding featured the matron of honor fainting and sinking to the floor during the middle of the ceremony. A quick-thinking pastor calmly stopped the ceremony, applied a cold cloth to the girl's face, and asked for a chair for her for the rest of the ceremony. Later he told the bride, "Don't be embarrassed. You had a unique wedding. Nobody else will ever have one just like it. You'll remember this always, with a smile." He was right. Other weddings leave my memory, but not that one, so a perfect wedding may not be all it's cracked up to be.

There are short, inexpensive weddings, and there are lavish affairs that leave one breathless. But neither one is guaranteed to be perfect, and even if one were, what about the marriage? The wedding doesn't mean anything if the marriage doesn't last. So the question now arises: What makes a perfect marriage?

Simple. There is no such thing. A perfect marriage involves the union of two perfect people, and that isn't going to happen. Perfection was definitely missing from my and Tom's union, but we've been married forty-seven years.

When Tom and I married, we called the justice of the peace for an appointment. He was waiting for us under a big oak tree in his front yard dressed in a khaki shirt and pants, and wearing bright red suspenders—but no coat and tie. He asked if we wanted a long or short ceremony. We said short. The ceremony went like this: he said, "Do each of you take the other to be your lawful wedded husband and wife?"

We both answered, "I do."

"I now pronounce you husband and wife."

A perfect wedding? Not by today's standard, but the marriage has lasted and even flourished. Most marriages last only a fraction of the time that ours has, but with a lot of work, a lot of love, and continued respect for one another, a marriage can last "till death do us part." That's what Tom and I are shooting for.

SACRIFICES
by Ibbie

I always knew my son would make a good husband, and was assured of it when his new bride said, "Tim gave up eating onions just to please me."

CLOTHES DON'T MAKE THE MARRIAGE
by Ibbie

Jerry asked his dad, L. C., to be best man at his wedding. This required L. C. to wear a tuxedo. Reluctant to get that dressed up, and saying that the groom ought to be best man at his own wedding, L. C. said, "When me and your mama got married, I just put on a clean pair of overalls, jumped on Old Blue [his mule] and went down to Beach Flatt after her. She swung up behind me, we rode by the preacher's house, and he married us standing under a big oak tree. We got us a drink of cool well water, got back on Old Blue, went to Mama and Papa's and stayed till the crops was gathered. And it's lasted thirty-five years."

Fifteen years later, at his mother and dad's fiftieth wedding anniversary celebration, Jerry had already been divorced. When he announced plans to marry again, L. C. said, "Son, this time you better wear a pair of overalls and go get her on a mule."

TREASURES OF THE HEART
by Johnnie

Hidden in the very back of a closet at my Aunt Ibbie's house was a worn footlocker.

Aunt Ibbie's big regret in life was that she and John, her beloved husband of fifty-five years, were never able to have children. Her sister (my mother) was blessed with ten children, so Aunt Ibbie became a second mother to all of us. She was so fun-loving and carefree. To spend the night at her house was a real treat in my childhood days.

She's gone now. When she passed away, it became my and my sisters' duty, or rather privilege, to go through her belongings. It was a cold January day when we started what turned out to be a sentimental journey.

Aunt Ibbie's last year was spent in a nursing home, so there was no heat in the little house that day. A steady snow was falling. The house contained many treasures; not much of monetary value, but treasures just the same. We felt sad with the knowledge that we'd be selling everything she had accumulated over a lifetime. We shivered, both from the cold and from the prospect of what we were about to do.

As we delved through her belongings, we discovered the trunk. I had spent many days and nights in her home, but had never seen it before. We dug it out, dusted it off, and held our breath as we quietly pried it open. We were all awed by its contents. Here we found the real treasures of Aunt Ibbie's life.

The house didn't seem so cold as we huddled around that old trunk. On the very top was a worn yellowed pillowcase with a homemade row of lace crocheted around the edge. We knew Aunt Ibbie must have made that lace herself. Inside the pillowcase was a fragile old Bible. Its cover was missing and the pages were frayed, dog-eared, and yellowed with age, but it contained so much precious information about our family roots that it immediately became priceless to us. It was Grandpa Lane's Bible, and the first entry was a notation made in 1881, the day he and Sara Burnham were married.

Every entry in that book meant something special to us. There was a lock of hair wrapped in cellophane. We had no idea whose hair it was, or why it had been kept, but we were sure there was a warm and loving story behind it. I picked up a bundle of letters tied together with a satin ribbon of pink, Aunt Ibbie's favorite color. I untied the ribbon, then quickly tied it back again. They were letters from John, written while he was away from home working. I couldn't invade the privacy of their love, so I didn't read the letters.

There were pictures of friends and family, as well as cards and letters Aunt Ibbie had saved for a lifetime. So much to look through and ponder over, but the trunk's contents were too valuable in sentiment to hurry through, so we decided to leave everything intact for a more leisurely time. However, as we were carefully closing the rickety old lid, something caught my eye. A closer look revealed Aunt Ibbie's wedding ring, a gold band with little diamond chips across the top. I was so excited! I just had to have that ring for a keepsake! To my relief, the others all said, "It's yours."

The ring is the only thing of value that's left now of Aunt Ibbie's worldly goods. The little house was sold, along with most everything else. I wear the ring and think of her often.

The old trunk with its treasures was left in my care. Someday, when time permits, I will savor its contents.

Aunt Ibbie left something behind that is more valuable than any of her physical treasures—her impact on all of our lives. I believe that God has a plan for every life, and that he used Aunt Ibbie's life to touch so many others. I know that in His eyes, and in mine, too, she was a great lady.

PEN NAME
by Ibbie

When I first began my writing career, it occurred to me, Maybe I should have a pen name. I've always been proud of my name, having inherited it from my beloved Aunt Ibbie; however, it's difficult for people to pronounce and spell.

So I began thinking of pen names that would be simpler for the public to grasp. Margaret McMitchell came to mind, but that wouldn't do—someone might confuse me with the author of *Gone With the Wind*. Maybe I could be Elizabeth Brownelle—but that's too similar to a name that has been taken. Then I thought about my nickname.

I didn't know my husband Willie's nickname for me until his company held a banquet for employees and spouses, and I was introduced to a group of his co-workers. One of the ladies said, "Oh, I'm so glad to finally meet 'Itchy Boo.' I've often wondered what you look like."

"Who's 'Itchy Boo'?" I asked. Willie sheepishly admitted that he called me Itchy Boo at work. I could tell Willie used the name only as an endearment, so I felt amused and flattered rather than embarrassed. I figured the name issued from the fact that I have very dry, itchy skin, so I often ask Willie to scratch my back. After I revealed my nickname to my co-workers, they too began calling me Itchy Boo. Soon, it was just Itchy.

One morning I called a girl who hitched rides with me to let her know I wouldn't be going in to work. Her dad answered and said she couldn't come to the phone. I said, "Just tell her to call Itchy." He got the message a little mixed up and told her to call Scratchy.

Guess I'll just stick with Ibbie.

A DATE TO REMEMBER
by Ibbie

Jim couldn't help admiring the beautiful girl who sat in front of him in his English Lit class. After about a month of hesitation he finally got up enough nerve to ask her for a date, which, to his surprise and delight, she readily accepted.

Wanting to make a good impression, he made reservations at the nicest restaurant in town. The waiter escorted them to their table in a secluded area. The table was covered with a crisp white cloth. A candle, surrounded by fresh flowers that Jim had requested, made the perfect centerpiece. Everything is just right, Jim thought as he seated Melony; however, as he proceeded to sit down himself, he noticed that his fly was unzipped. Without looking down, he hurriedly zipped up, hoping desperately that Melony hadn't noticed.

They had a very enjoyable dinner. There was definitely chemistry between them. Jim was feeling so sure of himself, so confident. When it came time to leave, Jim, being the gentleman that he is, rose from his chair and started around to assist Melony. The tablecloth moved with him. Dishes began crashing. He barely caught the lighted candle before it hit the floor. Had one of them stepped on the cloth, causing it to slide off the table?

Puzzled, Jim made another slow move, and noticed that with every move he made, the tablecloth moved likewise. Then, to his horror, he realized that the cloth was caught in his zipper. He pulled on the zipper and the cloth, trying in vain to free himself. The waiter finally located a pair of scissors and cut him free.

It took two weeks for Jim to get up enough nerve to call Melony again. He discovered she had not dated anyone else and had in fact been waiting, hoping he'd call.

The fly story will be one to tell their children and grandchildren, for Jim and Melony were married four months later.

Chapter 4

This and That

THE WATCH
by Ibbie

The pages of the Sears catalog were dog-eared and worn, especially the pages that showed watches. Twelve-year-old Willie Ledford had chosen one of those watches to wish for. He even cut out the picture and carried it around in his pocket. He did so want that watch for Christmas, but in reality he knew that Mama and Papa couldn't afford it, since there were six other children in need of gifts.

Christmas came. Willie got candy, fruit, and some fireworks. He kept the picture of the watch, and would often take it out and wish some more.

The Ledford family was enjoying the anticipation of spring when bad news came from California. The telegram said that an automobile accident had taken the life of Millard, Willie's sister's husband. Willie's sister Clara and the body would arrive by train in two days. The house was made ready, for in those days—the early '40s—the deceased was brought to the house.

Relatives and friends were waiting when Clara and the coffin arrived at the Ledford home. When the coffin was opened, Clara became hysterical, and her mother had a difficult time calming her. After the original shock was over,

Clara calmed down and the grown-ups backed away. Willie decided to take a look at the brother-in-law he had liked and admired.

As he peeked over into the casket, he got the shock of his life: Millard was wearing the watch Willie had been wishing so hard for! One just like the picture in the Sears catalog! Why was a dead man wearing *his* watch?!

The room grew quiet, except for an occasional sob. Willie sidled over to Clara and whispered, "Are ya gonna bury that watch with Millard?" This sent Clara into another fit of crying. Seems she had ordered the watch as a Christmas present for Millard. He had gotten to wear it only a short time, and he had loved it so. Mama scolded Willie for daring to mention the watch at such a delicate time.

Willie never got an answer to his question, but he felt sure that watch was as good as buried. He thought of sneaking up that night after everyone fell asleep and removing the watch from Millard's arm, but his fear of touching a dead person was much greater than his desire for the watch.

Willie still had slight hopes that Clara would see the foolishness of a dead man wearing a watch and would give the watch to him, but, as the casket was being lowered into the ground, everyone was crying, including Willie. They were actually going to bury his watch!

Willie probably grieved as long over the death of the watch as Clara did over the death of her young husband. Burying that beautiful watch made no sense at all to a twelve-year-old.

THE QUILTING
by Ibbie

While the other kids played outside, my cousin Dixie and I often sneaked in under the quilt to listen to the latest gossip. Often we heard things that were not meant for young ears, including the following:

Ms. Nina said, "L. H. caught Alma Marie behind the barn smokin' a store-bought cigarette. Seems she bought 'em when we went inta town. Bought a whole pack with the money I talked L. H. inta givin' her fer pickin' cotton. He paid the boys fer workin'; I didn't see why he shouldn't pay the girls. He said all along that girls don't have no business with spendin' money. Alma Marie has always been a rebellious child. Even when she minds she's got that rebellious look on her face. No tellin' what she'll get inta when she goes out in the world."

Ms. Emily said, "Frank had ta talk to the teacher 'bout Eugene. Seems he's been disruptin' the class with his shenanigans. We 'spicioned he was kinda struck on his pretty young teacher. She's boardin' with the Butlers, ya know? Mrs. Butler says they're real taken with her. Frank tried to make me jealous by tellin' me how pretty he thought she was, but I know fer true ain't no pretty little schoolteacher gonna take up with an old clodhopper like Frank." The other ladies laughed, while Dixie and I were barely able to stifle our giggles.

Ms. Bertha said, "Did y'all hear 'bout the fight over to the White Oak School dance? The way I got it, the Scroggins and Turner boys come over from Beach Creek and was cuttin' up and dancin' with all the White Oak girls. Some of the White Oak boys asked 'em real polite-like to leave. They said they jest might do that, and take the girls with 'em. One thang led to another—a shove here, a shove there—and the fight was on. The White Oak boys won out, seein' as how it was more of 'em, but several of the boys on both sides'll be sportin' black eyes fer quite a spell."

By this time Ms. Leona, the one lady not so skilled with a needle, would almost have dinner ready. Some of the menfolk who worked the nearby fields would come and take dinner with us. It would be time to roll the quilt, and there would no longer be enough room underneath for Dixie and me to hide undetected. After dinner we'd go to the hayloft in the barn and giggle ourselves silly, remembering the gossip we'd heard under the quilt.

THE MIGRATION
by Ibbie

Years ago during the lazy, hazy days of summer, the crops would be laid by and there would be time to visit the neighbors. Mama and the kids would walk down the dusty road to see Mona Fay and her brood. The boys would ride stick horses while the girls skipped along playing tag and trying to catch butterflies.

Upon arrival, Mona Fay and Mama would sit on the porch gossiping while the children played. The menfolk usually hung out at the country store, talking cotton and corn prices and just "shootin' the bull."

During this period of the year, our city relatives and friends would migrate our way. They would leave their fancy homes, drive out in their shiny cars, and delight in helping us feed chickens, hogs, and milk cows. They got the biggest kick out of gathering eggs and holding a baby pig or goat in their arms. They even enjoyed riding in the back of our old truck. The greatest thrill of all was crossing the fields in the wagon to swim in the river.

We were their poor relatives and friends, yet they inherently knew that we had something money couldn't buy: clean fresh air, wide open spaces, and the pleasure of seeing the fruits of our labors. Our guests would leave with gifts of fresh home-canned fruits and vegetables, a sack of eggs, and a jug of milk. And we'd bet they'd be back the first chance they got. They wouldn't find a better place to eat or sleep, not even at the fanciest vacation spots. Of course, there was a little bit of envy on both sides, but I do believe a farmer's life was the best of the two worlds.

"SANG HUNTIN'"
by Ibbie

Many people who live in the Tennessee hills supplement their income by hunting ginseng. "Sang huntin'," as the hill people refer to it, is much like searching for buried treasure. A big clump could be just over the next rise, so you hunt until you're exhausted or until darkness drives you out of the woods.

Not only is "sang huntin'" good exercise, but it's also very profitable, sometimes bringing as much as three hundred dollars per pound for the dried root.

Marge had hunted the three-leafed plant with its human-shaped root for many months. As each root dried, she placed it in a box in the storage room for safe keeping until the herb man appeared at the co-op in February to buy the herbs that had been gathered by the hill people. Marge had more ginseng this year than ever before, and figured that it, along with the goldenseal she had gathered, would provide a lot of much-needed cash for the family.

When the big day arrived, Marge got up early so as to beat the crowd of herb gatherers at the co-op. As she opened the storage-room door, she noticed a hole in the side of the box containing the precious "sang." She was afraid to look inside. Lifting the lid, her fears were realized. All that was left of the hoarded root were a few twigs. The culprits were revealed by the rat droppings in the box.

Big tears rolled down her face as Marge thought of the plans she had had for the money from the sale of the "sang:" bills that could be paid and new curtains for the living room.

Marge was no longer in a hurry to get to the co-op. After the initial shock wore off, she finally took her pitiful supply of goldenseal to the herb man, hoping it would bring enough money to buy a good batch of rat poison. But it's doubtful that any amount of poison would have been enough to kill those rats, for they had eaten pure, uncut ginseng! Ginseng is said to be very potent, giving strength, vim, and vitality to anyone—or anything—that consumes it. Those rats would make great specimens for a scientific study.

AUNT IBBIE
by Ibbie

Aunt Ibbie was a very special person in my young life; she was like a second mother to me. She was never able to have children of her own, but every child and animal with which she came in contact felt her motherly love.

She and Mama were sisters, and they married brothers. Mama and Papa had ten children, and it was only natural for Aunt Ibbie and Uncle John to help raise us. Aunt Ibbie did the cooking, washing, ironing, and loving when Mama had to take time off to have a baby.

Because she laughed a lot, Aunt Ibbie was called a jolly person. She was also a singer and a hugger. We often sat on the porch swing singing hymns and funny songs. When our son Steve was about ten years old, we were on our way to visit Aunt Ibbie. Steve's friend Donny was with us. Steve cautioned, "I gotta warn ya, Donny, Aunt Ibbie is gonna hug ya," and hug him she did. Even though little boys sometimes pretend they don't like a healthy embrace, all who came near Aunt Ibbie and got the treatment seemed to enjoy it.

Aunt Ibbie didn't have any biological children to remember her, but she will always be thought of with love by those of us who came in contact with her, and felt as though we were her kids, if only for a little while.

OUR BROTHERS CHOCK AND TOP
by Johnnie

Years ago, when we didn't have TV, nor even radio, kids and grown-ups alike had to make their own entertainment. That was easy to do in the large farm family of six boys and four girls in which our brothers Chock and Top grew up.

If you asked around in our community in Dyer County, Tennessee, who Charles Turner and Joe Robert Lock were, nobody would know. But if you used their nicknames, Chock and Top, then everybody knew who you meant.

Chock's nickname came from the fact that he had high cheekbones and Papa would say he looked like a Choctaw Indian. When Top was small, his hair was literally as white as cotton, so people referred to him as "Cotton Top." The name stuck. After awhile it was shortened to Top.

Being only two years apart in age, Chock and Top were inseparable. And they were always in trouble. Top was afraid of nothing; perhaps that's why he was run over by the first car that came to our community.

Our teacher showed up one day driving a new Model T Ford. She explained that we should stay out of her way when she drove the car. She said that if we got run over it most likely would kill us. The first day she pulled out of the school yard, Top ran along beside her. He was gaining on her and, giving a last big effort, passed catty-cornered in front of that old Model T. Sure enough, the crank caught his shirttail and knocked him down. The wheels of the car barely missed his body.

The teacher ran back, picked him up, brushed him off, and began to examine him. Top let out a cuss word and said, "Am I dead?! Am I dead?!"

Chock and Top played jokes on each other and on other family members almost daily. When the two boys were about seven and nine, they were playing behind the outhouse. They saw Papa coming down the path in a half-run.

He couldn't see them. Top said, "Watch this." He broke off a stick about a half-inch around and two feet long and stuck it up behind the toilet through a crack in the stool. He jabbed Papa with it where the sun don't shine. Papa jumped two feet into the air and ran out with his pants in his hand, yelling, "Snake bite! Snake bite! Go get Dr. Turner!" Of course that made their day, so they moved to the next thing at hand.

Chock and Top loved baseball. The local diamond was about a mile from our house. One day, when they were about five and seven, Mom dressed them in shorts and short-sleeved shirts that were starched and ironed to perfection, and they started off to the ball game. It was extremely hot that day and the dirt road was covered with dust. Ms. Minnie Vance and her teenaged daughter came by in their horse-drawn buggy. Chock and Top thought it would be fun to take hold of the back of that buggy and run along the rest of the way. Just as they got a good hold, Ms. Minnie gave Old Dan a whack with her buggy whip and they were off in a flurry of speed and dirt. After a few feet, Chock turned loose. He lost his balance and rolled about ten feet in the dirt. He got up and wiped his eyes just in time to see Top turn loose. They dusted themselves off and walked on down the road to the ball game.

It was just another day in the life of two country boys.

ONE LETTER WILL DO
by Ibbie

My sisters and I are very close and often invite each other to read mail that we've received from family members. When my sister Margaret moved and the phone company could not connect her phone service right away, our brother called from Detroit requesting her address. I said, "I know the name of the street, but not the number. If you want to write her, just send it to my address. We often read each other's mail, especially your letters." Chock replied, "Well, then, I'll just address my next letter to 'you all'."

IT'S ALL IN THE ADVERTISING
by Ibbie

When Margaret placed an ad in the local newspaper that simply said, I do alterations, she got very few calls. After rephrasing the ad, she got more sewing than she could handle:
Ripped your britches?
Need a few stitches?
Gave it a jerk and
Your zipper didn't work?
A stitch in time
Saves nine.
If you can't do it at your house, bring it to mine.

SISTERS WILL BE SISTERS
by Ibbie

At our Memorial Day family reunion, Margaret was dressed very appropriately in white pants, a red blouse, and a red, white, and blue plaid jacket. When someone complimented Margaret on her outfit, Johnnie piped up and said, "That's some of my old clothes she's wearin'. She got 'em at my yard sale."

Margaret said, "Well! The only reason you were sellin' 'em is you couldn't get 'em over your big fat butt!"

NUMBERS ARE GOOD
by Ibbie

Have you ever been fearful of forgetting your name? It can happen.

My sister-in-law Clara had just moved from California to a small town in Arkansas. While talking to a local grocery-store owner about her years in California, she wrote a check for the groceries she'd gathered. Several days later, she received her bank statement and discovered that the check was signed Clara California, the account number affording all the identification necessary to cash the check.

WHO'S COUNTING?
by Ibbie

Aunt Ibbie often corrected Uncle John's English.

One day while eating dinner, Papa passed the biscuits and said, "Have another biscuit, John." Uncle John said, "No thank ya. I done et four." Aunt Ibbie said in exasperation, "It's 'ate', John!" Uncle John conceded, "Well, maybe it *was* eight I et."

JUST CHASING AROUND
by Ibbie

Grandpa said he still liked to chase women, but if he ever caught one he'd let her go and give her another chance.

A GRAMMAR LESSON
by Ibbie

We once moved to a rural area where our nearest neighbor was about a mile away. The couple had several children. One day their six-year-old boy and eight-year-old girl came to visit. The little boy constantly used terrible grammar. I finally thought it necessary to correct him. I said, "Dwayne, you should say, 'I saw', not 'I seen'." His sister said, "Oh, Mrs. Ledford, he ain't got no manners. You can't learn him nothin'."

IT'S BAD

by Ibbie

I had just entered the grocery store when I came upon my friends Frank and Linda. They were frantically searching through their pockets and Linda's purse. "Have you lost your money?" I asked. "Worse than that!" Frank replied. "We've lost our list!"

MY SLIP WAS SHOWING
by Ibbie

While I was dressing for a dinner date, the black slip I intended to wear disappeared. I knew I had taken it from its drawer, but it was nowhere to be found. Willie was in a hurry, so I gave up the search and wore another slip.

We met two other couples at the restaurant. After we were seated, Willie began reaching for a menu when he noticed what he thought to be the lining of his coat sleeve hanging out. He began pulling on it, and it seemed that the more he pulled, the more fabric came out. I think the people around us thought he was a magician. Finally the trick reached its climax, and Willie held up the innards of his sleeve for all to see. It was the black slip! It must have been lying on Willie's coat when he put it on.

While everyone pretty much fell over laughing, I seized the moment to quickly grab the slip and stuff it in my purse. I never went to that restaurant again!

EIGHT-YEAR-OLD FORGER
by *Ibbie*

Beth was in the third grade and her work had always been excellent. One day the teacher sent a note home saying that Beth had not been handing in her assignments. Beth's mother, Maxine, asked her about it. Beth said she always handed in her work. Maxine believed her and decided she should talk to the teacher.

The teacher explained her procedure each morning to Maxine. As she called the roll, the children passed their homework papers up and the child in the front seat of each row put them on the teacher's desk. Beth was in tears and assured the teacher that she always passed her paper along with the others. This was a puzzling situation. The teacher said perhaps she had been distracted and would study the routine more carefully.

The next morning, as the papers were being passed up front, the teacher watched out of the corner of her eye and saw the little boy in front of Beth erase Beth's name, put his name on her paper, and pass it forward. She could hardly believe it. An eight-year-old forger! The teacher had wondered why his grades had improved so much. If he had just been smart enough to put Beth's name on *his* papers, poor little Beth might never have gotten out of the third grade.

OLD FOLKS NEED A KEEPER
by Johnnie

We began a small remodeling job at our house, doing the work ourselves. Ibbie volunteered to help paint, and right off the bat she moved a ladder with an open bucket of hunter-green paint sitting on top. It's a good thing we were planning to put down new carpet.

My husband, Tom, was wearing walking shorts, but no shirt or shoes. He had tied a work apron with pockets for nails and tools around his waist. So one of us was half-dressed, and the other two were a lovely shade of green.

We worked hard all day. Ibbie and I quit as the sun set, but Tom wanted to finish up his current project before calling it a day. I urged him to wait till tomorrow, since I figured that as tired as he was, there was no telling what he would do wrong. "Nope, I'm gonna finish," was all he'd say.

An hour later he came staggering into my office, appearing a trifle addled. Fussing and grumbling, he said, "I moved the ladder and my hammer fell off and hit me between the eyes. I guess I've injured my eyes really badly. Everything looks blurred. You look blurred." He was acting so strangely, I became very concerned. I said, "Lie down for a bit and see how you feel. You could really be hurt." Tom was scared, so he was easily persuaded. He lay back on the bed, closed his eyes, and handed me his glasses.

The glasses felt strange. Peering closer, I suddenly began to laugh. One lens was missing. Tom was not hurt at all. The falling hammer had hit his plastic-framed glasses, knocking the left lens out. His "blurred vision" was caused from looking through only one lens. We had a good laugh, and remarked how God takes care of those who can't take care of themselves. I'm glad we have a keeper.

HOW OLD IS OLD?
by Johnnie

My sister Margaret, age seventy-three, bought a house, financing it for the maximum of twenty years to keep her payments low. At the real estate closing, her young lawyer said, "Miss Margaret, you sure are getting a pretty house, but it's so small."

With no hesitation at all, Margaret answered, "Oh, that's okay. When I get it paid for, I'll sell it and buy a bigger one."

Mama was in her late seventies when she accompanied a young man to the cemetery to place Papa's tombstone. It was a double stone with her birthdate engraved on one side. The young man said, "I hope I'll have the privilege of writing the other date on yours someday, Mrs. Lock." Mama looked him up and down and said, "You look pretty healthy, son. Take good care of yourself and you just might outlive me."

What an attitude! Old is whatever one perceives it to be.

TRIBUTE TO A GREAT SINGER
by Ibbie

I was invited to play Trivial Pursuit with my children. Since most of the questions required knowledge of subjects I knew nothing about, I wasn't expected to be much help to my team. But one question did allow me to show the kids I actually knew a thing or two.

I got all excited when the opposing team drew the following question: Whose theme song was "When the Moon Comes Over the Mountain"? The other players, all under thirty years old, were stumped. I could hardly contain myself while I waited for the other team to admit defeat so I could answer. I remembered Kate Smith's theme song vividly.

Papa would often say that she was the only woman whose singing he enjoyed. Her radio program used to come on every day at noon. When Papa and the boys would come in from the fields for dinner, we would all listen. The program always opened with Kate Smith singing "When the Moon Comes Over the Mountain." She and her husband would talk about world affairs and give market, cotton, and corn prices. Then she would sing another song or two. "God Bless America" was Papa's favorite.

After the trivia game I decided I must find some of Kate's songs on tape. Now I am enjoying all of her oldies, and "God Bless America" has also become my favorite; it makes me feel very reverent and thankful to live in this wonderful country. Thank you and God bless you, Kate Smith, for giving Papa and me so much pleasure.

A SPECIAL LADY
by Johnnie

I called Trula to see if she had jotted down some information I needed to write her story. She said, "Hon, I haven't had the time. I've been working extra hours lately at Wal-Mart. I've had a house full of company to cook for, done my usual church work, and met with my circle. I haven't had an idle minute since you asked me to do that." Trula is eighty-seven years old.

The most admirable quality about this gracious lady is her attitude. I overheard someone forty years her junior say to her, "I think I'll give up all my church jobs next year and just rest. When are you going to retire?"

Miss Trula smiled and answered, "I didn't know you could ever retire from doing God's work." She teaches a Sunday School class and sings in the church choir. She regularly visits others on behalf of the church, and is usually the first person to appear at the door with food and words of comfort in times of trouble. Everyone values Miss Trula's friendship. She loves and accepts us all just the way we are. Miss Trula says, "I can say I've been truly blessed with a good, long life, and a wonderful family that is so good to me. I'm grateful for a life full of love: first, love from God my Savior and Lord, and then, love from my children and friends. I give thanks and praise every day to my Heavenly Father from whom all blessings flow." Miss Trula brings a ray of sunshine into the lives of all who know her. I, for one, give thanks to God for this true and dear friend.

COUNTING MY BLESSINGS
by Ibbie

It was a quarter to four, almost quitting time; however, since our department hadn't reached its quota for the day, the boss said, "Two hours overtime." Overtime would look good on the paycheck, but I was so tired. And I knew what awaited me when I arrived home. There was supper to prepare and housework to tackle. The kids and husband would need attention. Even the dog would be waiting for a pat on the head. All I wanted to do was sit down and put my feet up, have a cold drink, and ignore everything around me.

The two hours passed rather quickly and I was on my way home. Poor little me, I'm thinking. Supper will be late, so I'll have to listen to the inevitable complaints. I'll get the lowdown on everyone's day, though no one will ask about my day's adventure. By the time I finish and preparations are made for the next day, it will be ten o'clock. I'm thinking, Is it worth all the effort?

As I round a curve I've rounded thousands of times, my train of thought is suddenly interrupted. I pass this way every day and had begun taking the beauty of the area for granted. The lake, hills, and trees were always there, so there was no special reason to take note of the scenery; however, since I was two hours later than usual, a special reason was soon apparent. The sun was setting, creating an image of a huge ball of orange suspended over the lake. I stopped the car and gazed as the sun sank lower and lower, appearing to sink right into the water.

A humble feeling came over me. I thanked God for the many blessings He had bestowed upon me. He made me sit up and take notice of this beautiful world, a world I had taken for granted. I vowed that that would not be the case ever again.

ONE LIFE TO LIVE
by Johnnie

We came to know the Paris family at church. There was Edd, Betty, and their three boys: Mike, Billy, and Gary. Mike and Billy were teenagers, but Gary was very young. Over the years Betty and I became very close, drawn together by the first of many tragedies she suffered.

It all started on a Saturday afternoon. Our family was eating lunch when we heard a noise that sounded like a gunshot. Everyone paused to listen, then someone said, "It's 12:30. Remember the time in case we're asked later if we heard a shot." We continued with our eating and fun until we heard the haunting sounds of an ambulance and police car turning down our street, sirens screaming. We all ran outside to be confronted by the sight of a stretcher coming from the house across the street. A policewoman was standing on the sidewalk, and as I walked up beside her, we both gasped, recognizing the boy on the stretcher to be Mike Paris. We didn't know whether he was dead or alive.

The ambulance driver yelled for someone to get Mike's parents to the hospital as quickly as possible. The policewoman knew the Paris family also, so we both headed for the Paris's home some two miles away. When we arrived we found Betty washing dishes and Edgar drying them. They were laughing and joking together. We rushed in, both talking at the same time, and told them that there had been an accident involving Mike and they were needed at the hospital. Edd sent Betty with us because he knew she had to go. He stayed behind with Gary.

I don't remember much about that five-minute drive to the hospital, except that Betty never asked what happened. She just calmly and quietly prayed that God would be with all her family, and that He would help her accept whatever was ahead.

Betty could see only a little of the emergency room

through a crack in the door, but it was enough that she knew whose boots were showing from under the sheet on the stretcher. They wouldn't let her go in, though, and she felt fear and frustration. She pleaded, "Please, I'm his mother! I only want to hold his hand!" With a sad face the doctor said, "My dear, he can't feel your hand. Mike is dead." Betty cried out, "Help me Jesus!" And she heard Him quietly say, "I'm right here with you."

Betty said, "God touched me that day. He literally wrapped me in His arms. And He has kept His arms around me ever since."

Mike was dead on arrival, killed while he and his friends were playing with a gun that went off accidentally. He was fifteen years old.

Betty and Edd hurt badly, but they weren't bitter. They retained their faith in God. Their example touched everyone who knew them. We visited their home and saw them at church. We thought them to be brave and remarkable people to be able to withstand what they had gone through with such grace.

Less than two years later, tragedy struck again. This time Betty was sitting on the sofa in her living room when I arrived. She was calm once again. It was she who told me what had happened.

Billy and some friends were going to the river for a wiener roast. Betty had cautioned her son about how treacherous the Mississippi River can be, and she had received his promise that he wouldn't go for a wade or a swim.

The boys built a big bonfire on the bank. Then everyone except Billy went swimming. He lay on the sandy beach while his friends swam about, until he heard a shout: "Help!" One of his buddies was far from shore, caught in the strong current. Without hesitation Billy jumped in the river to save his friend. The friend made it to shore, but Billy didn't.

"I hope they find him soon," Betty said softly. "I can't stand knowing he's in that cold, muddy water." Three days later Billy's body was recovered.

She didn't blame God or the other boys. This time, as before, she and Edd comforted the boys involved and their parents. Again they were so brave and their example touched many lives. I couldn't understand it, and in prayer asked, "Why, Lord? How much more can the Paris family take?" But Betty, Edd, and Gary picked up their lives with a renewed spirit of love. We who were close to them shook our heads, not understanding this strength.

Soon after Billy's death Edd started feeling unusually tired. His stomach bothered him, and he had difficulty holding down his job. After several months the pain finally forced him to see a doctor. After extensive tests, the doctor spoke the dreaded word "cancer."

Our pastor went to the hospital to pray with the Parises, to try to lighten their burden a little. He was amazed to see Edd sitting up in bed enjoying an ice cream cone. With a big smile, Edd comforted his pastor, rather than the other way around. "Yes, I know the diagnosis, but not to worry," he said. "God is able to take care of it." Neither Betty nor Edd questioned the Lord, but I continued to do so, and asked again, "Why Lord?"

As cancer patients sometimes do, Edd would feel pretty good for a few days, then be really sick. Betty and Edd were so close. There was so much love between them. They lived each day to the fullest, and thanked God for giving them one more precious day together.

Only a few months passed before God's final call came for Edd. The day before he died, he told his pastor, "Betty and I are at peace. God is so good." Edd wanted to live. He wanted to stay here to take care of Betty and Gary. And as he drew his last breath, a big tear slipped down his cheek. But he died the same way he lived, knowing that God was in His heaven, and all was right with the world.

Betty says, "I miss all three of them desperately." Then she smiles as she talks about how happy they must be now: "The three of them together in that lovely mansion He promised. I don't have to worry about my boys now. I'm lonely, but oh so grateful. Thank you, Jesus."

Since Edd's death, God has used Betty, a very shy person, to help others. She said, "God knew I wouldn't heed His call unless it came in a dramatic way. I'm now ready to serve Him however and wherever He wants me." She counsels others who have lost a loved one. She speaks before groups of people, and gives her testimony to any church congregation that asks.

When Gary was fourteen, he often felt panicky about the approaching age of fifteen; however, Betty didn't overprotect him. Like Job, she continues to love and trust God in His infinite wisdom.

A DOZEN RED ROSES
by Johnnie

I awoke that long-ago morning with a strange feeling, a feeling I couldn't explain. Everything seemed fine. The sun was shining, the weather was wonderfully warm. The next day would be Mother's Day, and my mom was well and happy. So what was wrong? My best friend, Nadell, had been hospitalized for several weeks with a heart condition, but she had returned home within the last few days, apparently well on the mend. My world was in fine shape.

We went about our Saturday as usual. A leisurely breakfast, house cleaning, shopping, yard work. But the foreboding remained. It surrounded me like a heavy mist. Being a happy person by nature, that feeling simply had to go. I decided to walk down the street to visit Nadell.

We had lived as neighbors for years, and had been close friends since we had first met. Nadell is the kind of person to whom one tells their troubles, and she knows exactly what to say to make those troubles seem small, while making the person seem big and important. I chose not to let on that I felt blue, but I knew that talking with her would make everything right again.

As I walked down the street, I stopped to pick a bouquet of red roses from a bush in our yard. I knew Nadell would be pleased. When I arrived, she was sitting on the front doorstep still dressed in her pajamas and robe. A mischievous grin was on her face as we met. She said, "Come on in. I'll put these roses in water. I want to show you what I got today."

Sitting on her living-room table was a dozen long-stemmed red roses, a Mother's Day gift from her son, Tommy. I had never seen any roses as pretty as those. They made my offering look small, but she seemed just as pleased with mine. She exclaimed, "I've never had roses before, but today I got two bouquets. Makes being sick almost worth it. I know the sacrifice Tommy made to pay for these, and I keep pinching myself to make sure I'm awake."

I fussed good-humoredly that she already had a Mother's Day gift, while the rest of us had to wait another day.

Nadell spoiled her children, but at the same time she had molded them into beautiful human beings that left the nest to have families of their own. Nadell was so proud of her kids.

We had a nice visit. She said, "For a while there I was afraid I wouldn't live to see Mother's Day this year. But now I believe I'm gonna make it. I feel really good."

That night we were sound asleep, but when the phone rang, I grabbed it right away. That strange feeling awoke within me. I knew that whatever I had dreaded all day was on the end of that phone. A man's excited voice said, "Both of you come down quick!" That's all he said, and the phone clicked. I looked at the clock. It was 11:30. We couldn't leave our children home alone, so Tom rushed over. When he called five minutes later, his voice was but a whisper: "She's gone, hon. John [her husband] refuses to believe it. What can we do?"

When I arrived at Nadell's house, she was sitting in her favorite chair gazing at her roses, with a lovely smile on her face. Her last minutes had been spent enjoying the happy feeling of owning—for the first and last time—a dozen beautiful long-stemmed red roses.

TOMORROW MAY NEVER BE MINE
by Johnnie

"Yesterday's gone, sweet Jesus, and tomorrow may never be mine." This beautiful old song rang out as we sat in our church sanctuary saddened by the death of a dear friend and Sunday School class member.

Jean had looked younger than any of us; she had appeared to be in excellent health. Just a week ago she'd been at her regular place in our group. She had recently returned from a trip to Hawaii, and was all aglow as she related how beautiful the islands were and how much she enjoyed the trip, saying it was like heaven on earth.

By the next Sunday Jean was gone. Her chair was empty. It's hard to describe our feelings. It seemed as though a large hole was taking up half of the room. How did it happen?

On Wednesday, Jean had developed a terrific headache. The pain had become so severe that her daughter persuaded her to see a doctor. The headache had quickly worsened, and Jean's doctor knew she was in serious trouble. He sent her in a helicopter to Memphis, where they pronounced her brain dead. I don't know all the details, but Jean died late that Friday afternoon at the age of sixty-three.

None of us felt like discussing the Sunday School lesson that day, although it was appropriate for the occasion. In that lesson one verse of Scripture told the whole story: James 4-14: "Whereas ye know not what shall be on the morrow. For what is your life? You are even a vapor, that appeareth for a little time, and then vanisheth away."

"Yesterday's gone, and tomorrow may never be mine." We all felt that way. Bobbie asked what we thought Jean would say to us now if she could. June said, "I think she'd tell us to keep on plugging along."

Someone else said, "I think she would say, Friends, come on home. It's beautiful and tranquil here."

Personally, I think she would tell us to savor every moment we have together. To love one another and to strive to be more like Jesus. I think she would say, Make very sure you know the Lord, so that when you finish your labors on Earth, you can come home to this unspeakably beautiful place.

Yes, I believe if Jean could speak to us today, she would tell us that Hawaii's beauty doesn't even hold a candle to where she is now.

Chapter 5

Live and Learn
(Bits of information learned from our combined 126 years of living)

FIRST, CHECK IT OUT
by Ibbie

Having heard so many commercials singing the praises of calcium, especially for those of us who are considered senior citizens, my husband and I decided to take one calcium tablet a day, which is the recommended dosage. Within a week, we both became irregular—an uncommon condition for us.

As I was leaving for a meeting one day, Willie said, "You'd better buy a laxative while you're in town." I went to the meeting before going to the drugstore and discovered that we probably didn't need a laxative after all.

The speaker at the meeting was a local pharmacist with a message and literature about over-the-counter drugs and their side effects. I learned that one of the side effects of too much calcium in the body was constipation, so I didn't buy the laxative.

We simply stopped taking the calcium tablets and our problem worked itself out. Now, we check all available literature before taking any kind of medicine or vitamin, even those prescribed by a doctor.

THOU SHALT NOT JUDGE
by Ibbie

I had no patience nor sympathy for people like my neighbor Mary, who always seemed moody and unhappy. I would think, She could be happy if she really wanted to be!

Although my family didn't have much money, our needs were met, and we enjoyed the simple pleasures in life. This gave me happiness, and because I was happy, I became very smug in my belief that one could control his or her emotions and choose to be happy or unhappy. This led me to judge too harshly those who were depressed, especially Mary, who often came to me for encouragement when she was down. I'm convinced God led me through a depressed time in my life in order to make me more humble and understanding.

I don't know exactly when it started. Maybe it was when my beloved Uncle John passed on, soon after we had moved away from family and old friends. Yet, I had no big problems in life. I had a good husband and a sweet son still living at home. Why, then, except as God's punishment for my arrogant ways, was I subject to feelings of unhappiness and despair?

Something had to be done; trying to fight the depression alone was not working. I needed help. I went to our family doctor crying like a baby, pouring out my feelings of depression and the shame I felt for feeling this way. I also explained my thoughts on the matter, that only people with great tragedy in their lives should be depressed.

Dr. Turner was kind and understanding. He assured me that it would be difficult—in fact almost impossible—to overcome these feelings alone, and that he was going to help.

After he ran some tests on me, he explained that the changes taking place in my body had caused a hormone deficiency, and that feelings of depression were not uncommon for a woman who was forty-five years old. He gave me a shot and a prescription for hormone pills, and assured me that I'd be my old fun-loving self again when my hormone level stabilized. Within an hour I could tell a difference; I felt as if a load had been lifted from my shoulders.

I still have periods when the old depressed feelings come back to haunt me, but they only last a short time. I try always to be aware of my many blessings; I am thankful that there are wonderful doctors like Dr. Turner, who helped me retrieve my happy life. If anyone reading this story feels depressed and hopeless, please get help. A physical disorder may be the cause. Don't while away the days in despair. Life on this beautiful earth is so short and sweet. Don't waste a minute of it!

WHO'S MINDING THE STORE?
by Ibbie

Suffering excruciating pain from a kidney stone attack, I called my doctor's office and was told to check into the hospital for treatment. Dr. Moore would make the arrangements and see me when he made his rounds that afternoon. I did as ordered.

Seven o'clock rolled around and there was still no sign of Dr. Moore. I was suffering terribly, so the nurse got permission to give me a sedative, and I drifted into a fitful sleep.

Sometime during the night I went to the bathroom and passed the stone. I awoke feeling fine, expecting Dr. Moore to come by and release me. When eleven o'clock arrived, all the other doctors had finished their rounds but Dr. Moore had not come. I called his office, informing his nurse that I was okay now and only needed to be dismissed. She put me on hold, came back, and said, "Dr. Moore says you should stay in the hospital one more night to be sure there's no infection. He'll be in to see you when he makes his rounds."

I agreed to stay.

When the doctor didn't show up for evening rounds, I called his answering service, only to be told that he had left that afternoon for a week's vacation and had turned his cases over to Dr. Turner. "Dr. Turner will see you in the morning," they said.

When morning rounds were made, and Dr. Turner didn't show, I called his office and was told, "Dr. Turner's mother died last night and he's out of town."

I checked myself out of the hospital without ever seeing a doctor, owing a bill of several hundred dollars that my insurance didn't cover!

TICKED OFF
by Ibbie

I once cut short a camping trip at the lake in order to spend some time with Agatha, a long-time friend of mine who, being a city dweller, was quite unacquainted with the country life. While I was driving to her house, a nagging itch developed in the center of my back. Just barely able to reach the area with my fingertips, I figured it must be a tick. Ticks are smart little critters; they know exactly how to plant themselves just out of reach.

Agatha greeted me with an affectionate hug; however, I was almost pushed back out the door when I pleaded, "Please look on my back. I think there's a tick on me."

"A tick! A tick!" she cried. "Get outside! I've never had a tick in my house!"

"I can't go outside, Agatha! I have to take off my blouse and you have to get the tick off. The little son-of-a-gun has sucked himself right into the center of my back out of my reach. Just take these tweezers," I explained as I opened my first aid kit, "and pull it off."

Agatha raked the tweezers across the tick, saying, "I've never taken a tick off anyone before. I don't know how."

"Just get a good hold on it and pull."

The tick finally let go and as Agatha held it—bloated with my blood—captive between the tweezers, she asked, "What shall I do with it?"

Her little granddaughter Jennie said, "Let me see, Granny! I want to see the tick!"

As Agatha held it down for Jennie to see, she released her grip on the tweezers just enough for the tick to fall onto the carpet. Agatha screamed. Jennie screamed and ran behind the door. We looked for the tick in the deep-piled carpet, but couldn't find it. I said, "Don't worry. The vacuum will pick it up."

"Are you sure?!" Agatha yelled. "I don't want a family of ticks living in my carpet!"

I assured her that without a mate there would be no "family of ticks" in her carpet, and that even if the vacuum didn't do its job, the tick would soon die.

Poor Agatha! In her whole sixty-five years she has never been camping. She's never had a tick on her. She's never known the soothing relief of rubbing an itchy tick bite with a cotton ball drenched in alcohol. She's never experienced the friendly looks and licks of appreciation from a German shepherd after you've pulled the ticks from his ears.

Agatha has missed so many heartwarming experiences by being a city girl. Never having had an encounter with a tick is just one of them.

Note of caution:

This is a fun story; however, a tick bite can be serious. Ticks carry diseases such as Rocky Mountain spotted fever, Lyme disease, relapsing fever, Q-fever, bullis fever, Colorado tick fever, and a Western variety of sleeping sickness. If after being bitten by a tick you develop a fever or rash, see your doctor and tell him you've been bitten. The diseases carried by ticks are often hard to diagnose if the doctor isn't aware of the bite.

THE WOODPILE
by Ibbie

Many of you may have heard the expression, "Stay out of your neighbor's woodpile." In the days when wood had to be cut with an ax or handsaw, and was the only means of keeping the family warm, a man's woodpile was indeed a very important part of life. It took much hard work to supply a family with enough wood for the winter, so messing with a man's woodpile wasn't taken lightly; thus, the phrase "stay out of your neighbor's woodpile" has become a synonym for not messing with anything dear to a person's heart.

During the early 1940s, everyone in our area burned wood for heating and cooking. Wood was plentiful; all that was required was a good ax, or the loan of one, and a strong back. When my brother-in-law Robert began to miss wood from his woodpile, he was determined to catch the lazy good-for-nothing. A man who was too lazy to cut wood to keep his family warm and to keep food on the table was not going to get away with stealing wood from Robert.

Robert bored holes in pieces of the wood, filled the holes with gunpowder, and placed the special wood right on top of the pile. It wasn't long before it became evident who the thief was. A neighbor's stove blew up, catching his house on fire and burning it to the ground.

For years nobody, except Robert, knew what could have happened to make that stove blow up. When his boys grew into teenagers, even though wood was no longer the main source of heat, Robert 'fessed up, saying, "Boys, let that be a lesson to you when you're tempted to mess with another man's woodpile."

I OUTWITTED A COMPUTER
by Ibbie

After receiving a catalog in the mail containing very revealing lingerie and sex-play items, I called the company to inform them that I would not be ordering merchandise from their catalog, and I asked that my name be removed from their mailing list.

Two weeks later the same catalog arrived; this time it was a sale edition. The explanation I received was that perhaps the cancellation had not yet been processed through their computers.

About six weeks later another catalog arrived. I was embarrassed for the mailman to know I was receiving it. I even wrapped the catalogs in heavy grocery bags when throwing them away so the garbage men wouldn't see them.

Writing the company did no good. The catalogs just kept coming. I don't know how my name got on their mailing list, but it seemed it was there to stay.

Then an idea came to mind. I thumbed through the latest issue of the catalog and found a change of address form. I looked in the yellow pages of the nearest big city, filled in the form with the address of a warehouse, and mailed it in. The catalogs stopped coming.

Maybe a night watchman at that warehouse is whiling away the lonely hours enjoying one of those catalogs. I hope I didn't get anyone in trouble, but I just had to get rid of those catalogs. And I'm pretty proud of the fact I outwitted a computer.

WE MUST BE CAREFUL
by Ibbie

It was a beautiful spring day. The wooden door to our front foyer was open. The glass storm door wasn't locked, as the lock had been broken for some time.

When I heeded the ring of the doorbell, a young man, neatly dressed in casual attire and his hair pulled back in a ponytail, stood there smiling at me. I said, "Hello," without opening the glass door. He introduced himself; not being able to hear very well with the door between us, I thought he said he was the new neighbor who had just moved in two houses down. So I opened the door and shook his extended hand.

As he talked, he mentioned magazines and the points he would receive toward a scholarship if he were able to sell them. I didn't see any magazines or any other papers in his hands. I asked, "Did I understand you correctly? Are you our new neighbor?"

He said, "No. But I do live in the area."

When I let him know that I wasn't interested in buying any magazines, he said, "Ma'am, I'm so hot. Could I have a glass of water?"

A light went on in my head, and I thought, Is this just a ploy to get me away from the door? Is he going to push his way in? As I hesitated, he said, "I'm so thirsty. I've been going door to door, and I sure would appreciate a drink of water."

I said, "Wait here," as I quickly pulled the storm door to and made the motion of locking it. My husband called out, "Who was that at the door?" I answered loudly, "A nice young man who wants a drink of water," hoping to allay any suspicions I may have aroused in the young man. I didn't want to make him nervous.

I got the water. As I pretended to unlock the door and handed him the glass, I felt very uneasy. I said, "Just leave the glass on the porch," slammed the wooden door shut, and bolted the lock, leaning against the door in relief. I watched through the bedroom window and noticed that he didn't stop at any other house.

Maybe the young man was okay, or maybe his hearing my husband's voice or believing the door was locked saved me from a terrible fate. We see such horrible true stories on the news every day. It's such a shame that the days have passed when we can't invite a person into our home for a cool drink of water. Instead, we must be so careful.

DON'T GET YOUR DANDER UP
by Johnnie

Our preacher said he had watched, in his rearview mirror, some fellow travelers who were stopped behind him at a traffic light. He said he often observed troubled people on the highways.

The couple in the car behind him was obviously in a heated argument. Their lips were moving rapidly, their hands were waving, their faces were frowning—all body language that seemed to indicate anger. Wondering if he could help, our preacher was tempted to get out of his car and walk back to offer a word of encouragement. But he didn't. So he did the next best thing: he turned around in his seat and stared at them. This action so distressed the young woman that she placed her head in her hands and wept.

Watching people behind me is a pastime that I also enjoy. I can peer at them in the rearview mirror without the other person knowing. I once noticed two adults fighting tooth and nail while stopped, but as soon as the light changed they immediately stopped their hitting and drove merrily on down the road.

I used to have a pet peeve, which I turned instead into a delight. When traffic is heavy, and it seems as though there will never be an opening in which you can merge onto the lane you're seeking, the person behind often makes matters worse by first beating on the steering wheel, then loudly blowing the horn, urging you to move on. That bit of rudeness used to make me steaming mad; but not any more.

Now when I hear that first toot of the horn, I turn around and flash a great big smile and give an enthusiastic wave, pretending that I'm waving to friends. With every beep of the horn, I wave more vigorously and smile more broadly. They tap the steering wheel harder and look even more grim. But at least I don't meet anger with anger, so I avoid aggravating an already tense situation. This fun-loving performance from me sure makes rearview watching more interesting, and provides a happy environment for driving.

LUNCH ON THE HOUSE
by Johnnie

Ibbie and I were frantically working on our latest hobby when Tom walked through and matter-of-factly said, "Here's two free lunch tickets. You two have lunch on me today." The tickets were from a place which made fancy sandwiches and salads. I had eaten there once before and didn't care much for the food. But it was free, so we were going.

It's not often one gets a free lunch these days, so as we readied ourselves we felt great about our good fortune. When we arrived at the restaurant, we presented the tickets and asked what we could order from the menus.

"Anything you want," was the reply.

This was great! We both ordered the biggest sandwich on the menu, and the preparer said, "You each get a bag of potato chips. Help yourself." Oh boy! It just kept getting better!

"A free drink comes with this meal deal," the young man said. "What kind do you want?" We looked at each other, smiling broadly. I chose a big orange drink, and Ibbie got a cola. The cashier took our tickets, punched several keys on the cash register and said, "That'll be $8.82."

"But we gave you two free tickets."

"Oh, no. The lunch is not free. The ticket reads, Free drink with meal."

Deflated now, I slowly explained, "We thought the whole lunch was free."

The cashier just stared with a blank expression, his cash drawer hanging open. A long line was waiting behind us; everyone could hear our conversation and was shifting impatiently from one foot to the other. In a calm, low voice, I said, "We're disappointed, and you don't even care, do you?" He still didn't say a word, nor change his countenance.

We paid the money and sat down to eat, then met each other's eyes and burst out laughing. We spoke at the same time and said, "I'd rather have had a hamburger for a lot less money." From now on we'll believe the old sayin', "There's no such thing as a free lunch."

ARE FLYING SAUCERS REAL?
by Johnnie

I often get out of bed in the middle of the night and go to my office at the far end of the house, simply for the pure joy of sitting alone enveloped in darkness, with only my own thoughts for company.

During one such night I was sitting alone as usual, thinking and gazing at the ink-black sky lit by a trillion stars. The moon wasn't out, and although the stars were legion, they gave off very little light. Suddenly I noticed an object hovering over our neighbor's house two doors away. Its shape consisted of an elongated center with tapering sides. It appeared to be metal and looked kind of like pictures I'd seen of the Stealth bomber. The object shone brightly, though not continuously; instead, at systematic intervals, it would glow with light similar to a spotlight on trees at Christmas. There was very little movement, except when the object brightened. Then it seemed to move up and down slightly. No noise at all issued from the craft.

I watched for about thirty minutes, then woke my husband Tom. He watched with me for some twenty minutes, then said, "I don't know what the heck it is, but I'm goin' back to bed." I couldn't believe his lack of interest in what seemed to me a once-in-a-lifetime opportunity to actually observe a UFO.

The object continued its hovering maneuver at no more than ten feet above my neighbor's house. Finally I decided that I just had to see that UFO close-up, but not alone. Tom wasn't interested, so I called the police department. I said, "I'm not crazy, or drunk, or on drugs. You're going to think I'm under the influence of something, though, when I tell you why I'm callin' at three o'clock in the morning. I've been sitting here in my home for over an hour watching a UFO hover over my neighbor's house. I want to go outside for a closer look, but I'm afraid. Could you send someone out to go with me?"

The dispatcher didn't even hesitate. Although I was calm, she became excited. She said, "A patrol car will be there momentarily." True to her word, five minutes later the car pulled into my driveway with lights out.

We stood in my driveway some two hundred feet away from the object, intently watching for a few minutes, but the policeman could see nothing. I could make out the outline of the object, but he couldn't. I assured him it would light up soon. And it did, staying lit for a few seconds, then dark again. Now he, too, could make out its outline. We stared quietly for at least ten minutes, both of us in awe of what we were seeing. The way it lit up without any pattern at all puzzled us. He whispered, "Let's walk over closer to get another angle."

We walked to the yard next door, putting us about 125 feet from the object. Again, we could only see the outline at first. We whispered back and forth as if the thing could hear. It soon lit up again, and we both said in wonder, "Well, I'll be."

We suddenly knew what our UFO was. There was a four-lane highway about an eighth of a mile away. Cars and trucks traveled it all night long. Standing closer to our target, we realized that every time a vehicle passed down the highway, its lights shone on a huge metal satellite antenna on my neighbor's rooftop. That was our "flying saucer"!

THINK, THEN DON'T!
by Johnnie

I knew exactly what was wrong . . . the trouble was a broken alternator belt. Our service station attendant had warned me that it was frayed and that I should replace it before going out of town again. I didn't have time for repairs right then, and I had promptly forgotten about it. Now here I was, my car broken down on a lonely stretch of highway with darkness about to fall. One consolation, though—I was not alone. My good friend, Rheba, was with me. We had been shopping in Memphis.

We decided that she would stay with the car, guarding our purchases, while I walked about a half-mile down the road to a nearby farmhouse to call home.

I was only a few yards from the car when a young man driving a pickup truck stopped and said, "I see you're having car trouble. I'm an off-duty policeman, can I help?"

"No, thanks, I'm just going to that house to ask to use the phone."

"Hop in, I'll give you a ride."

The day was hot and humid, with not even the slightest hint of any breeze. I was already sweating profusely, so the prospect of a ride in an air-conditioned truck sounded great. Without asking for any identification, I gratefully accepted his invitation.

We exchanged a few pleasantries, then I got out at the house. I knocked on the door and a teenager, who looked to be more than six feet tall, opened the door.

"My car is broken down. May I use your phone to call home? I'll reverse the charges."

In a sullen manner he mumbled, "Yes, ma'am."

He followed me down a narrow, darkly-lit hallway, pointing out the phone. He stood nearby staring at me as I talked. I reached my husband, Tom, and he said he'd come get me and bring an alternator belt. I thanked the boy, hurriedly brushed past him, and practically ran out the door . . . a little uneasy now, realizing that in less than an hour, I had invited not one but two potentially dangerous situations. How lucky, or blessed, can one be?

Looking back, I'm thankful for that experience. It made me much more aware of possibilities to be in harm's way. Let's all be careful. Think about what you're doing; if it seems dangerous at all, then don't do it.

WE CAN'T PICK A TIME TO BE SICK
by Johnnie

Until recently, I had been blessed with remarkably good health, other than a few colds and a couple of minor operations.

The exception is my spring and fall allergies. May 1993 brought the usual coughing and wheezing again. I stocked up on over-the-counter medicines as usual. They seemed to be working well until one particular morning when, around five o'clock, I awoke choking. I jumped out of bed and ran to the bathroom, trying to cough up the phlegm in my throat. The harder I coughed the worse my breathing became. Eventually there was no air getting through. I began issuing a loud wheezing noise, a sound I had no control over. I thought I was dying.

Tom heard the commotion and came to my rescue. By this time I had almost passed out, turning a deathly gray. The look of horror on Tom's face confirmed my fears. I thought, Lord, I'm coming home.

Tom literally dragged me down the hall, across the living room and foyer, and outside. The cold morning air shocked my system into taking in a wee bit of air. I sank down on the front steps, and little by little inhaled more of that cool, fresh air. Several minutes passed before my breathing and color returned to normal.

I didn't go to the doctor. My dad had had a bad case of asthma in his later years, so I concluded that my allergies had turned into asthma. I would just have to tough it out until the spring pollen left; then I'd get better. I was afraid to lie down, however, for fear I'd quit breathing again. So I spent several nights of fitful sleep in a chair, continuing to choke several times each night.

On May 4, at about ten o'clock at night, I went to sleep in my chair, then began choking. I was wheezing and coughing again. This time I rushed to the front porch, and this time it took longer to get my breath back. I was scared. Sitting there on my front porch stoop in my nightie, I decided to see a doctor as soon as possible.

My sister Ibbie was visiting, and said that she would go with me. I would make an appointment with a doctor in Jackson who had treated a friend for the same ailment—or so I thought.

How naive can one be? I picked up the phone and called the doctor's office, only to be laughed at when the receptionist understood that I wanted an appointment that day. She said, "We only take referrals from other doctors. Have your family doctor contact us." This meant two sets of office calls and two sets of tests instead of one—a totally unnecessary expense in my mind. I said, "But this is an emergency. I'm afraid that tonight when I go to sleep I'll have another spell and choke to death. You treated a friend for the same symptoms and she referred me to you."

"We can't help you. Sorry." Bam! She hung up the phone. Now I knew I had a real problem on my hands. I hadn't seen a doctor in ten years, and that doctor had died about five years ago. I decided to call a young family practitioner, a neighbor I'd known for many years. I figured that since he was a new doctor, he might not be too busy yet. His office clerk said, "He's booked up for three weeks."

"I'm sick. I can't wait three weeks."

"Sorry."

"Don't hang up!" I yelled. "I've known Jim since he was in high school. He lives right down the street from me. Please ask him if he will see me today."

"I can't do that," she answered. "Several people he knows have already asked to see him today and he's said no every time."

"I really need a doctor *today.*"

"I can make you an appointment for three weeks from now."

"I could be *dead* in three weeks. Thanks but no thanks."

Next, I got dressed and went to a medical clinic. They would see me, but would not take Medicare and supplemental insurance. I would have to pay the bill—an $85 office call plus a $90 X ray—out of my own pocket, with no hope of reimbursement from my insurance company. Apprehensive about what might be wrong with me, and the fact that it could lead to all kinds of expensive bills, I decided not to pursue treatment at the clinic. I had paid insurance companies good money for many years for just such an emergency; I intended to use that insurance now.

Still optimistic, I thought, I know what I'll do. My kids see a family doctor who's been in practice only a short time. I've referred numerous people to him, including my own kids. I've helped him build his patient load. He'll see me.

Wrong! His office clerk asked what kind of insurance I had. "Medicare, plus a supplement."

"We aren't taking any new Medicare patients," she replied.

"But I have supplement plan F, 100 percent coverage," I informed her.

"We can't help you."

"I've known Dr. Brown ever since he came to town. I've recommended patients to him when his practice was slow. I'm really sick. Can't you at least ask him?"

"Nope." She hung up.

There I was, sick and scared, and no longer optimistic, wondering what to do next. I called my neighborhood doctor's office again. He's associated with several other doctors in the same building. Maybe one of his colleagues could see me. A different girl answered the phone. I asked to talk to the girl with whom I had spoken before. In a cool voice she said, "Who did you speak with before?"

"I don't know her name. My name is Johnnie Countess. Can't you ask in the office who talked with me a few minutes ago?"

"What kind of insurance do you have?"

"I already told the other girl. Can't I speak with her again?"

"Lady, I'm trying to help you. How old are you?"

"Please! I'm sick! Let me talk to the girl. I know your staff is not so big that you can't find out who I just talked with."

She didn't answer; she just placed me on hold for about five minutes. Finally the first girl with whom I had spoken came back on the line. In an irritated voice she said, "Dr. Mosta has had a couple of cancellations today. Would you like to see him?"

"Okay."

"I'll ask him." I heard silence and assumed that I had been put on hold—but it was not so. In a minute the dial tone sounded. I guessed that she had accidentally cut me off. Wrong again. I redialed and got a different girl from the first two. "I'm Johnnie Countess. I was talking with someone a minute ago and got cut off. May I speak with her again?"

"To whom were you talking?"

"She never gave me her name."

"What kind of insurance do you have?"

"Please! I've gone through all this with another girl in your office. Let me talk to her again."

"How old are you?"

"Sixty-five."

"What seems to be your trouble?"

I wanted to say, You. Instead, I said, "I've already told another girl all that. My name is Johnnie Countess. Can't you ask around the office and find out who talked with me a second ago?" No reply; just silence—I was on hold again.

After what seemed like an hour, the first girl came on the line. She sounded cross. "I didn't put you on hold, Mrs. Countess. I hung up. I will have to ask Dr. Mosta, then call you back."

"You didn't tell me that."

"Well, I'm tellin' you now." Bam! She hung up.

I sat there feeling helpless. Pondering what to do next, I remembered that my friend Judy had worked as a secretary for Dr. Omar, the last doctor I had seen, ten long years ago. Dr. Omar's son had taken over his father's practice, and Judy had stayed on as office manager. Maybe she could get him to refer me to the chest specialist I wanted to see in Jackson.

I told Judy my story on the phone and how I wanted to see the specialist. "You can't possibly get a same-day appointment to see any doctor, Johnnie."

"I have to. I'm really sick, Judy."

After a brief pause, she said, "Wait a minute. I'll ask Dr. Omar." She put me on hold, came back, and said, "Dr. Omar said okay. I'll try to set it up; I'll call you right back." True to her word, she called back shortly. "Dr. Johnson can see you on the thirteenth."

"No, Judy. I have to see someone today. I'm afraid when night comes I'll smother to death. Should I go to the emergency room now?"

She said, "I hate to see you do that. Let me talk to Dr. Omar again." Dr. Omar allowed her to refer me to another chest specialist in Jackson, who could see me at 12:20 P.M. the same day! I might barely make it there.

I was ecstatic! Judy gave me the doctor's name and the name of his clinic, which was located behind the hospital. Ibbie said she'd go with me, and we took off.

We arrived in Jackson about twelve o'clock, and drove down every street behind the hospital without finding the right clinic. I thought I saw a sign at the far end of a street with the correct clinic name. We drove up, parked right in front, and saw they were tearing the building down. I could see someone sitting behind a desk inside, so I went in and asked about the Jackson Westside Medical Clinic. "I never heard of it," she answered.

Another girl overheard us and said, "Oh, I think they moved that clinic way out on the bypass." Ibbie and I started laughing. Here I am, sick, not knowing what kind of report I'll get if and when I ever do get to see a doctor, and we're laughing. Those girls thought I was sick in the head. "If I'm late the doctor won't see me," I said between chuckles.

We left and drove over in front of the hospital. Glory be! We saw the clinic with five minutes to spare before my appointment. I filled out papers for thirty minutes. The questionnaire was more interested in my parents' health, or lack of it, than in mine. I thought for sure it would be necessary to exhume both my parents' bodies before getting in to see the doctor.

At about one o'clock I was ushered into a back waiting room and asked to put on a paper gown I couldn't close. I waited. I was so exhausted by now that the wait was welcome. The doctor came in smiling and full of enthusiasm. "What's the trouble, Mrs. Countess?"

"I can't breathe at night. I think I have asthma."

"And why do you think your problem is asthma?"

"My dad had it pretty bad. I saw him have spells like I'm havin'."

The doctor ordered a cardiogram, X rays, breathing tests, blood work, a blood pressure test, and some other tests. He listened to me breathe, said he would read my tests, and then left, promising to be back. Forty-five minutes and $800 later he did come back, and said, "Danged if it ain't asthma." Well, he didn't put it quite that way.

He gave me an inhaler and some medication, and that did the trick. I slept in my bed that night for the first time in several nights.

Attention everybody: Go to a family doctor before you need one. If you don't have a family doctor, and you do have an emergency sickness, you could die waiting.

SCHOOL DAZE
by Johnnie

Past fifty, but still feeling young at heart, my friend Margie decided to go back to college to prepare for a career in nursing.

She didn't have a problem with learning the material that she went there to study; her problem was unlearning the stuff she thought she already knew. Margie soon found that college kids in the '70s no longer spoke the same language nor dressed the same way they had some thirty-odd years ago.

First off, Margie learned to attend class in un-ironed clothes, with uncombed hair and an unwashed face (no makeup at all), and to wear faded, threadbare, tight-fitting jeans.

Students appearing this way were considered "cool." Margie's and my generation had always been cool, but we didn't know it. We dress in our old clothes at home, looking cool, and we thought we were just being comfortable.

Margie thought that "far out" meant "a long way off." Not so . . . it means "popular." She even had the notion that "grass" was the green plant growing in her yard and that "pot" was a cooking utensil. She also found out that "speed" does not mean driving eighty miles an hour, and "high" is not the top of the Empire State Building.

She thought that Century 21 was a real estate company and that Checkers was a game. She learned that these places are clubs where the far-out, cool crowd goes to party.

My friend also knew that the *Webster's Dictionary* definition of "gay" was "having or showing a joyous mood."

Margie remembers when ladies blushed if they were embarrassed. Now they are embarrassed when they blush.

A good family movie in Margie's day was all about well-adjusted families doing wholesome things together. Now family movies seem to show their audiences how to start one.

She believes that the sexual revolution is finally here and she knows she is completely out of ammunition.

There is one old expression, "laid back," that Margie will never allow the cool crowd to change for her. She says, "I will always go home at night, kick off my shoes, put on my cool clothes, and lie back in my easy chair for a well-deserved rest."

Margie gave up college after the first quarter. By the time she had learned the lingo of that bunch, they had been replaced by preppies. Rather than try to understand them, she decided to "bug off."

Chapter 6

We're Thinking

FOOD FOR THOUGHT
by Johnnie

Our life, from cradle to grave, is one long series of choices and attitudes. We have the power within our minds, regardless of the choices we make, to react to those choices with either a happy or a sad attitude.

I had a neighbor whose husband got a big promotion which required relocating the family to another city. Ann was reluctant to leave her hometown; in fact, she refused to go. Their happy marriage was being tested. I said, "Ann, you should give Jiles this chance. And Ann, your attitude, if you should agree to go, is most important. You can go and be happy and excited about making a new life for your family, or you can go and hate every minute of it."

Ann replied, "Then I would choose to hate every minute of it."

Ann would not budge. That was thirty-five years ago. Jiles was never given another opportunity to advance within his company. At retirement, he still held the same job he had started with, but he seemed to always have a broad smile on his face and a zest for living.

You see, Jiles also had two choices thirty-five years ago. If he took the promotion, he lost his family. If he stayed put and felt bitter, he lost his happiness. So Jiles, even though he did sacrifice the job opportunity, chose a happy attitude instead of a bitter one. Ann and Jiles can't go back and do it all over again, but there are those out there who have yet to be confronted with such a dilemma. Remember, choices are not nearly as important as your attitude once the choice is made.

OVER THE HILL?
by Ibbie

Not me—I'm still climbing. To me, over the hill has always been at least fifteen years older than I was at the time. When I was fifteen, I thought that thirty was over the hill. When I was twenty, I believed it to be thirty-five. At age twenty-five, I just knew that forty would be the end.

Well, I'm in my sixties now, and I'm still climbing the hill. And I don't plan on falling off the top for many years to come. It seems the further up I go, the better the view gets. Mama once said that she wasn't going to grow old, she was just going to turn into an old gray mare.

BRAIN DEAD
by Johnnie

Margaret locked her keys in the car the other day while coming to visit Ibbie. Ibbie wasn't home, so Margaret let herself into the house and called me, asking for the whereabouts of a locksmith. I said, "Margaret, you don't need a locksmith. Get a coat hanger and stretch it out. Bend a small crook on one end, find a window that's opened a little, work the coat hanger inside, and pull the latch." In a matter of minutes she was back in her car.

The next day she did it again; this time too, it happened at Ibbie's. Ibbie was busy watching TV and Margaret didn't want to bother her, so she grabbed another coat hanger. This time she worked and worked without success. During a commercial break, Ibbie yelled out the front door that perhaps Margaret should try the other door. Margaret walked around the car to discover the window was down.

She felt kind of foolish about what had happened, but at least now she knows how to approach such a dilemma. First she'll check both doors and windows, and then if that doesn't work, she has a sure-fire solution. She told us, "I'll just keep a coat hanger in my car, so that if I'm away somewhere and lock my keys in again, I'll at least have a coat hanger with me."

Good thinking!

GOOD DEAL
by Ibbie

Willie says that since he turned seventy he has no problem getting a lifetime guarantee on *anything* he buys.

YOU COULD BE NEXT
by Johnnie

Dr. B.'s whole manner was grim as he walked into the little cubbyhole where I was waiting to hear my test results. This visit was my third one. After the first round of testing, Dr. B. had said that my symptoms pointed to a well-known disease, but since he didn't think a gray-haired grandma was a likely candidate for that particular kind of health problem, more tests were needed before he could make a final diagnosis. He asked odd questions like had I ever had a blood transfusion? and was I totally faithful to my husband, and him to me? I answered no, then yes twice, to those questions.

Dr. B. had done more tests the day before, or perhaps he did the same tests over again. Now he stood facing me with an unbelieving frown on his face as he said, "After all the testing, I still don't believe you have AIDS." It took a few seconds for that sentence to sink in.

"What did you just say?"

"I can't believe you have AIDS."

I had always said that AIDS carriers, no matter how they contracted the virus, should be placed somewhere together and away from healthy people, like lepers in a leper colony. Suddenly this noble notion of mine confronted me. I had never thought that I would contract the disease.

I snapped back from my trance to hear Dr. B. ask, "How did you get the virus?"

"I don't know. I've never come in contact with HIV. I don't even know anyone personally who has it. I just can't have AIDS."

Dr. B. shook his head sadly and said, "There's an island in the tropics set aside for all AIDS patients. The law says you must go there. Please start making preparations to spend the rest of your life on that island, away from your family and all other healthy people. The AIDS patrol will pick you up this afternoon."

"But what about my family?! Can't I at least tell them good-bye?!"

"No, you can leave a note."

"A note?! Will I ever see them again?!"

"No."

I awoke drenched in sweat, and thanked God that it was only a dream. My whole outlook on AIDS-infected people is now different. Now all I have to do when I start to stray is ask the question, What if it were me?

PRIME THE PUMP
by Johnnie

Unusual occurrences often happen at sunrise; late risers miss so much.

I was up at five-thirty one morning, sitting on the patio, sipping my coffee, when the numerous birds in the yard began suddenly to chatter. Their voices rose and fell like people's, and I decided that they were actually conversing with one another. The birds became more and more excited, and the reason for all the chatter soon became apparent.

A baby sparrow had fallen from his nest. To make matters worse, a big Siamese cat had appeared, strolling leisurely across the yard. He slunk through the grass, shaking the dew from his paws as he went, his eyes fixed on the little bird. As he neared, the birds' conversation increased and sharpened in pitch. All kinds of birds, not just sparrows, were swooping down on the cat in an effort to divert him. There were cardinals, robins, and even loud and mean blue jays helping in the rescue.

The cat circled the baby bird a few times, licking his lips all the while, and dodging as best as he could the frantic attack of the adult birds. Soon, however, there were too many attacks to dodge, and the fight became so one-sided that Mr. Cat threw in the towel and ran for his life. He didn't even take time to shake the dew off his paws.

After witnessing this drama, I began thinking of how people ought to be like those birds. We can disagree and even squabble among ourselves, but when one of our neighbors falls, we should all rally around him or her, swooping down on the problem till it goes away.

A few minutes later I went inside and turned on the TV. A woman was being interviewed by a reporter, and she did a unique thing. She began pumping the handle of an old-fashioned water pump she'd brought along, saying,

"Pretend it's a hot July day. You and I are out for a walk and we pass this pump a mile or so down the road. We want a drink of cool water. In order to get that water, we first have to prime the pump.

"Life is like that," she continued. "In order to get something out of it, we must first put something into it. Prime the pump."

So many people today want to drink cool water, but they sure don't want to prime the pump. They want someone else to do all the work. All some folks want to do is to have their fill.

I turned off the television, closed my eyes, and leaned back in my easy chair. I could literally feel the peace and quiet all around me. As I lay there, I thought about what had just taken place in my backyard. That tiny mother sparrow had started the prime, and then her friends had helped her pump. Once the pump kicked in, they all worked together to save her baby. Half-asleep, I began to sing, "When I'm worried and I can't sleep, I count my blessings instead of sheep." I sat up with a start, realizing that at six-thirty in the morning, with my mind fresh, it was the perfect time to count my blessings, which are legion. My pump is already primed.

Life really is like an old-fashioned pump. For every cup of water we put into it, we get back anywhere from one cup to ten thousand gallons, depending on how long and how vigorously we are willing to pump the handle.

GUARDIAN ANGEL
by Johnnie

Watching the movie *Ghost* got me to thinking. Some of us ordinary people believe in the supernatural, meaning that we believe we are blessed with a real honest-to-goodness guardian angel who looks out for us. I confess to being one of these people.

Many times an unexplained feeling of well-being takes over when problems in my life seem insurmountable. For example, I have always had night blindness when driving after dark. To be caught on unfamiliar roads at night is a nightmare for me.

One stormy night while traveling alone on a strange four-lane highway, the rain began coming down so heavily that I literally could not see but a few feet past the hood of my car. I became so alarmed that I began hyperventilating. Afraid to pull over and stop for fear someone would plow into me from behind, I pressed on slowly and nervously.

Fact was, it seemed no one else was on the road. No other car lights were in sight, coming or going. Aloud I said, "Lord, you promised to take care of children and dingbats. I fit both categories. I'm your child, and it's really stupid of me that I allowed myself to be so far away from home at night, knowing the storm is coming, and knowing that I can't see to drive at night even when the weather is good. Please help me now."

Immediately, from out of nowhere, a car approached from behind. It quickly overtook my snail's pace. Instead of passing, though, it pulled alongside, even with my car. Its headlights penetrated that pitch-black darkness, lighting the highway far beyond my headlights' range. I couldn't tell what kind of car it was; I could only make out its outline. It slowed to my exact speed, driving side-by-side with me.

At first I was a little scared, but then I began to relax. The rain was still coming down as strongly as ever, but I could see. Would you believe that that car stayed right with me for many miles, until I was traveling on familiar roads close to home? Then the car turned off onto a seldom-used side road and was gone.

Maybe it was some kind person, sensing I was a senior citizen in danger, who simply wanted to help. But I believe it was the Father looking after His child, just like He promised.

Chapter 7

A Bit of History (Our brother's experience in the Gulf War)

DESERT STORM
by Johnnie

My brother Don was a member of the Tennessee National Guard, MP Company 269, in 1991 when the Gulf War began. But since he was fifty-four years old, we never expected him to be called into service. His company had been preparing for this mission for six weeks, but we thought that Don would be exempt because of his age.

However, there was a great need for mechanics, and Don was very experienced in that area. When the family learned that he would be leaving Fort Campbell for Saudi Arabia on January 26, we were devastated. We had lost one brother, in World War II, and we didn't want to lose another.

Don tells the story:

"After twenty-seven hours of flying, the company finally arrived at King Fahd's military airport in Da Haran. We were to be transported to an area for three days' rest. The twenty-minute bus ride took us to Cohbar Towers.

"A very luxurious apartment complex built by King Fahd, it was meant to serve as free housing for the nomads of his country; however, the nomads had preferred roaming the desert to living in luxury. The eight-year-old facility had never been occupied, so King Fahd had loaned it to the

U.S. military. Each floor had three apartments. My apartment consisted of three bedrooms, three baths, a kitchen, a separate dining room, and a den. All the fancy trappings escaped my notice at first, however, as all I was interested in was a hot shower and sleep.

"We stayed at Cohbar Towers for nearly three weeks. Our first three days were for rest and relaxation, as promised. The remainder of the time was spent cleaning equipment and scouting the desert, where we would later set up camp.

"We left Cohbar Towers by platoon units (twenty-five people). We and our equipment were transported into the desert on flatbed trucks. Each platoon set up their tents for sleeping and secured the area with barbed wire. Operations tents, with radios and other communications equipment, were set up, as well as a library tent and a rec room tent with a TV and games. The U.S. military did its best to provide all the comforts of home.

"Camels roamed the desert and proved to be pests. The barbed wire kept them from entering the camp, but the flies they attracted were awful, and there was no way to get rid of them. Blowing sand was also a big problem. Most of the roads were paved, but the sand, disturbed by moving vehicles, made for poor visibility. It was difficult to keep a vehicle on the road. We often lost sight of the road and got stuck in the sand on the side.

"We were about one hundred miles from the battlefield when the ground war began. Our job was to secure and guard any enemy prisoners-of-war. One day we had eight POWs; the next day, fifteen thousand. When the prisoners arrived, they were tired, hungry, and dirty. They were given food, water, and medical attention, and were provided with showers and a comfortable place to sleep. I could feel only compassion for them.

"I received word on March 21 that my brother Top had passed away. Although time would not allow me to attend the funeral, I was given emergency leave to go home. It was a sad homecoming, but a joyful one as well. I was mighty glad to be back home.

"In April I received a call informing me that my wife and I had been selected to attend a dinner party in Washington, D.C., hosted by President and Mrs. Bush. Dick Cheney and General Colin Powell would also be in attendance. All arrangements would be made for transportation and lodging.

"Not only was it an honor to be chosen to represent my company, but to have a chance to meet the president and other such dignitaries was really exciting. I was instructed to wear my class A uniform, and my wife Geneva was to wear casual evening wear. Geneva was very flustered, and spent a sleepless night and a day of frantic shopping trying to decide what to wear.

"Our instructions were to report to a room at the Washington airport where we would meet with other military personnel flying in for the dinner. From there we were transported together to a checkpoint, and then on to our designated hotels. We had expected to be escorted around the city in style, maybe even in a limousine. Instead, a green army bus was our transport to the exclusive Washington Hilton Hotel, where we stayed and where the dinner was held.

"Several hundred National Guardsmen and their spouses from all over the U.S. attended the dinner. Famous performers entertained, and Dick Cheney and General Powell spoke. But we were disappointed that President and Mrs. Bush were only able to join us by video.

"The trip to Washington was exciting and an honor, but we were glad to get home and return our lives to order. Being involved in Desert Storm and all that was associated with it is an experience that will forever be part of me."

Chapter 8

Christmas Memories

HILL COUNTRY CHRISTMAS
by Ibbie

Hill Country Christmas
With cabins all alight,
And fresh-cut cedars
Strung with popcorn and red berries bright.
Chicken in the oven;
Country ham a-boilin'.
Lots uv kin comin';
Nothing will go a-spoilin'.
Grace will be said
Thanking God up above,
For all the good vittles
And family love.

HOME FOR CHRISTMAS
by Johnnie

Many years have passed since I was home for Christmas. As the season approaches, I long to see Mama, to feel her loving arms around me, and to hear her say, "It's so good to see ya, hon. Welcome home." But I know it will never happen again, and I cry.

We've put up our tree—maybe the prettiest one we've ever had—sporting all its store-bought decorations. Mama would have been proud. Her old-fashioned Victorian angel-topper sits once again on the very top. When I climbed the ladder to place it there, I could actually feel Mama's love just as if I were a small child again, with her holding me high over her head to place that same angel on our tree. The angel's dress is a bit faded, but I had washed and ironed it, giving her whole countenance renewed brightness.

What would I give to taste Mama's made-from-scratch fresh coconut cake once more! I make one every Christmas, but it never tastes as good as Mama's.

Our kids are grown, with homes of their own. They'll be with us, and we'll be observing our own traditions, different from Mama's. I miss the noise of our big family all gathered at Mama's house on Christmas Eve. I miss sipping homemade boiled custard and eating all the goodies her loving hands had prepared especially for us.

The things Mama taught me were so valuable. Why did I always take everything for granted?

Christmas Day is nearing its end now. I saw Ibbie and Don today; I will see Margaret tomorrow. Brownie and Chock are too far away, so I won't see them, but Ibbie said she talked to them both this morning. They are fine, surrounded by their children and grandchildren. Top, Wallace, Little Tom, and Austin are in heaven with Mama and Papa. That fact gives me some comfort.

I am both sad and happy remembering yesteryear. Sad because I guess I never got over being Mama's little girl, and tonight I long to be that little girl once more, going home for Christmas to Mama and Papa. But I am happy because Mama is in that beautiful, carefree place with Him, and I know in my heart that I will get to be home for Christmas with her again someday.

OUR MOST PRECIOUS GIFT
by Ibbie

Lois, in the last days of her pregnancy, was not well, and had spent the previous couple of months in bed. I had tried to do my part by taking care of her two children, Kathy and Mike. One morning Lois's mom called with the announcement we'd been waiting for: Lois was in the hospital with the baby on the way! She asked if I would keep Kathy and Mike. Excitement filled the air as we anxiously awaited news of the arrival.

Though we were certainly concerned for the welfare of Lois and the baby, the burning question at the time was, Will it be a boy or a girl? Back in those days one didn't know in advance what the sex of the child would be, and that lack of knowledge just made the event all the more exciting and suspenseful. However, our excitement was short-lived when Lois's mom came by to pick up the children. She brought the devastating news that God had taken their baby brother to live with Him in heaven; they could not hold him or play with him as they had planned. Their baby brother had been born dead.

I could only imagine what a heartrending experience this was for the family, especially Lois, who had carried this baby for nine months with so much excitement and anticipation. I tried to be the proverbial "friend in need," allowing her to pour out her feelings and cry on my shoulder, and then assuring her that time would heal all; however, as time passed and she remained depressed and continued to mourn, my patience grew thin and I began to avoid her. I simply could not understand how she had developed such strong feelings for a child she had never known; a child she had never even held in her arms.

Eventually, although our children still played together, Lois and I saw less and less of each other. My life was full. Willie and I had two beautiful children—a girl and a boy—

and we didn't plan to have any more. Since the children were in school, I at last had some time to myself. Maybe I'd even look for a job.

After checking out job possibilities and filling out several applications, I was finally contacted for an interview. The interview went well, but before I could be hired, I was required to take a physical. The doctor said that I was in excellent health, which was satisfying to hear. Then he said it was his opinion that I would most probably have a perfectly healthy baby.

"What do you mean, 'healthy baby'?!" I cried. "I don't intend to have any more children!" Surprised at my outburst, he said, "Lady, you're pregnant!"

There had to be some mistake. I had had a very light period the previous month, but I never suspected I was pregnant. There had been no morning sickness as was the case with my other children. It was all so difficult to believe and hard to accept. When I told Lois, she said, "Please forgive me, Ibbie, but I wish it were me." To my horror I blurted out, "I wish it were you, too, Lois," quickly covering my mouth with my hand, unable to really believe I could say such a thing. But we already had our family. Our youngest was already seven years old, for heaven's sake! How I hated the thought of starting over with diapers, bottles, and sleepless nights.

An entirely uneventful pregnancy ensued. I felt great, but was never quite able to enjoy the excitement of a new baby, even after a surprise baby shower. My due date was December 24. I wouldn't even be home with the family for Christmas. What an inconvenient time to have a baby! Try as I might, I could not shake the resentment I felt about the intrusion of a baby into this time of my life.

While I was shopping for the groceries needed for Thanksgiving dinner, a nagging pain began in my back; it continued well into the night. A heating pad finally eased the pain and enabled me to sleep. I awoke about six in the morning, got out of bed, and started to the bathroom, when a liquid began flowing from my body. My water had broken! This really frightened Willie and me since the baby wasn't due for another month. Willie called Dr. Shelton, who said, "Get her to the hospital immediately!"

A neighbor came to stay with the children, and we began our wild ride to the hospital through rush-hour traffic. It seemed this baby was determined to interrupt one of our holidays; if not Christmas, then Thanksgiving. We were expecting a large family gathering at our house for Thanksgiving dinner. I had already purchased all that food!

Dr. Shelton was waiting for us when we arrived at the hospital. After examining me, he said that I was definitely in labor, but there was no reason to be alarmed. The baby's heartbeat was strong. By this time the labor pains were fifteen minutes apart, and the doctor said our baby would be arriving in about two hours. Now all the resentful feelings I'd harbored toward this baby came back to haunt me. How could I have allowed myself to think such thoughts? Why had I ever thought a baby could ruin our Christmas or any other holiday? I began to think what a sad Christmas we would have if the baby didn't make it, and I asked God to please let this be a healthy child.

As the pains intensified, I was heavily sedated. Sometime in the night I was awakened by someone shaking me. The little man with gray hair sitting on the side of my bed said he was a pediatrician; Dr. Shelton had called him in to examine the baby. I was still very groggy; the nurse standing beside Dr. Shelton seemed so tall that her head almost touched the ceiling.

I was told that I'd had a boy. I asked if my little boy was okay. The doctor said that his lungs were heavily congested, but he was big for a premature baby—more than six pounds—and that if he made it through the night he would probably be all right. I drifted off to sleep, not at all concerned.

About two in the morning I woke up with a start. I immediately felt my stomach with relief. I had given birth. It was over: My baby had been born. Then my thoughts shifted to the pediatrician's late-night visit. Had it been a dream or was something wrong with my baby? Willie should be here with me! Where was Willie?! I summoned a nurse and asked, "Where's my husband?"

"He went home to see about the children. He tried to wake you before he left."

"Is my baby okay? I want to see my baby! Bring me my baby!"

"We can't. He's in an oxygen tent and we can't bring him out."

I began crying and became hysterical. The head nurse was called. She explained that the baby had had congestion in his lungs, a common disorder with eight-month-old babies, making it difficult for him to breathe on his own.

I still insisted on seeing him. He was mine, as much mine as my other two, though I had yet to see him. The nurse gave in, saying that if I felt strong enough, they would put me in a wheelchair and take me to the nursery window. No problem; I would crawl if I had to.

The ride down the corridor seemed to last forever. My baby was rolled up to the glass, the only one in the nursery with an oxygen tent over his face. He was blue, and I could see his little chest heave with every labored breath. How could I bear it if he didn't survive? He'd been a part of me for eight months, and now I knew that I wanted this baby; I wanted him desperately.

Back in my room, I began thinking of Lois. I felt that God must be punishing me for being so selfish. For now, I understood the pain she had suffered with the loss of her child. I prayed that God would allow my beautiful baby to live, not only for my sake, but also to give him a chance to grow up and make a difference in the world around him, as I was sure he would.

Our prayers were answered; after five days, we got to take our Tiny Tim home. For most of the first night, I stood watch over his crib for fear our little miracle would stop breathing. The following night his grandmother stood watch. After a week or so we began to relax and enjoy our beautiful baby. No other gifts were necessary that Christmas. We had received the most precious gift God could bestow—a baby to love and nourish.

Today that six-pound "preemie" is taller than six feet, and his very presence is an everyday blessing to his dad and me. He is the child who takes time to pamper and humor us as we grow old. And he's also the gift of wisdom that allowed me to understand.

EDD RAGAN WAS A FINE MAN
by Johnnie

I remember seeing Papa cry only three times: when Little Tom died, when Wallace was killed during World War II, and over an act of kindness by Edd Ragan.

I was ten years old. I awoke around midnight to see a lamp burning on the kitchen table. Leaving a lamp burning up kerosene without anybody using the light was an unheard-of waste in those days of the depression. Thinking that perhaps the last person going to bed had failed to blow out the lamp, I got up to do the job; however, something didn't seem right as I tiptoed through the living room and into the dining room.

I stopped dead in my tracks, shivering. The fire in the fireplace had died down, but that was not the cause of my chill. I could see Papa sitting at the kitchen table, alone, with his head in his hands, crying. Having no idea what earth-shattering thing had happened to cause Papa such grief, I didn't know what to do. Sensing that to comfort him would only prove embarrassing, I felt that the only thing left for me to do was to steal quietly back to my warm bed.

But I couldn't sleep. It was two days until Christmas Eve, and earlier that night I had had visions of Santa arriving with his usual bag of goodies: fruit, candy, nuts, and one special gift for each child. My wish this year was for a pair of roller skates. Ibbie wanted a doll that opened and closed its eyes. Wallace had asked for a hunting rifle. The remaining siblings were already married with homes of their own. Now, as I lay there in my worried state, all I wanted this Christmas was for whatever was bothering Papa to be mended. I finally fell into a troubled sleep.

The next morning, everything seemed so normal that I thought maybe I had been dreaming, but I knew better. I was old enough to know that we had suffered crop failure two years in a row due to drought. We had barely made enough to pay our farm rent and to pay back the bank loan, with nothing left for extras. Sensing that Papa's problem was money, or the lack of it, I shyly told him that I really didn't want any skates, and not to worry about fruit, nuts, and candy. They weren't very good this time of year anyway. Papa smiled sadly, patted my head, and simply said, "We'll see."

Like always, our neighbor, Mr. Ragan, came over the night before Christmas Eve to wish Mama and Papa a merry Christmas. Mr. Ragan worked for the railroad, and had no children left at home. Observing the way the Ragans lived—in a new brick house, driving a new car, and never wearing homemade clothes—we kids thought they were rich. I heard Mr. Ragan ask Papa what the kids were getting from Santa. Papa, a proud man, lifted his head high and said, "The kids say they don't want anything this year, Edd."

Mr. Ragan quipped, "Oh, is that so? I never heard of Christmas without at least one present from Santa. Johnnie, I heard you say the other day you'd like a pair of skates. Have you changed your mind?"

"Yes, sir."

"Ibbie, what kind of doll would you like if you could choose any one you wanted?" Ibbie's eyes lit up as she described her dream doll. "Have you changed your mind, too?" Mr. Ragan continued.

She hung her head, looked up through her lashes, and said, "Yes, sir."

"Where's Wallace?" Mr. Ragan asked.

"He's out huntin' with a sling shot," Papa answered with a nervous laugh. Mr. Ragan left, shaking his head.

Christmas Eve was strange that year. Like every year past, Mama baked a country ham that Papa had cured. She killed one of our hens and prepared chicken and dressing, made numerous pies and cakes, and prepared a big container of boiled custard, using milk from our cows and eggs from our chickens. She didn't sing as she worked—

which she usually did—but she didn't complain, either.

On Christmas Eve afternoon, Mr. Ragan came by in his car and called Papa outside. They talked for a few minutes. I heard Papa say, "I've never taken a handout before, Edd."

"I knew you'd feel that way, George." He handed Papa a piece of paper and said, "Everything's listed here. You can pay me back someday." Papa got in the car and they drove out to the barn, driving all the way inside. Shortly, I saw Mr. Ragan's car leave, and Papa returned to the house laughing and crying all at the same time, not realizing anybody had seen or heard what had just transpired. He said at least a dozen times that evening, "Edd Ragan is a fine man."

The atmosphere was different now. We talked about tomorrow being the birthday of Jesus, and that it was He who should be remembered this night, not us.

"Time to go to bed," Papa announced cheerfully. I was too young to know exactly what I had seen and heard, so I still was not expecting Santa that night. Ibbie and I slept together. We awoke extra early Christmas morning, whispering back and forth for awhile, wondering why Mama had left the lamp burning in the living room. Ibbie was only six years old, and she fully expected Santa to leave her the doll, even though she had said she wanted nothing. I knew differently.

Finally, against my wishes, she stole out of bed. Immediately she let out a joyous scream. "Johnnie, I got the doll! I got the doll! Come here! You got sumpin', too!"

To my utter disbelief, there was the best pair of roller skates money could buy, with my name on them. Wallace had a hunting rifle. There was a warm robe for Mama and a pair of insulated boots for Papa. Santa had brought twice as much fruit, nuts, and candy that year. I didn't understand it then, but I do now.

I found the paper many years later among Papa's personal belongings, marked paid in full. The crops were good the next year, so Papa had been able to pay him back.

Mr. Ragan hadn't really wanted to be paid, but he'd known that Papa had to do it.

Edd Ragan was a fine man! George Lock was a fine man, too!

MAMA AND AUNT IBBIE'S SHENANIGANS
by Ibbie

The pranks Mama and Aunt Ibbie constantly played on one another were one of the delights of my growing-up years.

Whenever the family had fried chicken for dinner, Mama and Aunt Ibbie would cry out in unison, "Save us a back!" assuring us that the least-liked piece of chicken was in fact their favorite piece. I've since wised up to their plan, concluding that they were just trying to free the rest of the family from guilt while we devoured the best pieces, because by the time Mama and Aunt Ibbie had finished waiting on the table, the back pieces were usually all that was left.

When Mama cut up a chicken she left the tail attached. She and Aunt Ibbie truly believed that to be the best part, and called it the "sweet bite." During one meal this led to the sweet bite scuffle.

Aunt Ibbie had just sat down to the table and had fixed her plate. The piece of back she had on the plate, with its tail sticking up, was especially brown and crispy. Mama walked by, reached over, and said, "I want this," pinching off the sweet bite. Aunt Ibbie yelled, "You come back here with my sweet bite!" and the chase was on.

Mama quickly popped the sweet bite into her mouth and began dodging behind our chairs. Aunt Ibbie caught up with her and tried to make her spit it out. All this time Papa, Uncle John, and us kids were laughing our heads off. Papa finally pulled them apart and admonished, "You girls beat all, scufflin' over a chicken's hind end. Now sit down and behave yourselves." That made us laugh even harder. As you can see, we weren't always as well-behaved as the Waltons were at the dinner table.

Aunt Ibbie, determined to get back at Mama, starched Mama's drawers. And so the shenanigans went on. They were all done in fun, and they were never meant to hurt each other's feelings. The following prank could have hurt Aunt Ibbie's feelings, however, if not for Mama's gentle heart.

It all started when Aunt Ibbie left an old pair of shoes at our house. She had worn them while helping Mama in the garden. They were stuck back in a closet and forgotten.

A couple of days before Christmas, Mama discovered the shoes. She thought how funny it would be to wrap them up as a Christmas present for Aunt Ibbie, so she placed the mud-caked shoes in a large box, wrapped the box with red tissue paper, and tied it with a big green yarn bow. She created a pretty card trimmed with lace, and inscribed, To my dear sweet sister Ibbie. I know this gift will make you very happy. Love, Eva. Mama set it under the Christmas tree.

Mama and Aunt Ibbie were always so busy preparing for the holidays, what with making gifts for the children, cooking, and otherwise thinking and doing only for family, that they never exchanged gifts between themselves. When Aunt Ibbie asked who the gift in the large box was for, Mama answered, "Look at the card, but don't pick it up." Aunt Ibbie got excited when she saw her name on the box, and exclaimed, "Oh, Eva! You shouldn't have gotten me a gift. I don't have anything for you."

"Oh, don't worry about that, Ibbie," Mama said, barely able to stifle a giggle.

On Christmas Eve, as Mama and Aunt Ibbie baked pies and cakes and worked together to make everything ready for Christmas Day, Aunt Ibbie began trying to guess what was in the box. She knew it had to be something that Mama had made, because there was no money to buy anything. She said, "The box is so big. I can't imagine what it could be. Is it a crocheted bedspread or shawl?"

"Nah," she answered herself, "it couldn't be. You couldn't do that much crocheting without my knowing about it." Then she suddenly cried, "Eva! Are you giving me Mama's tulip quilt? If you are, I won't accept it, because I know how much it means to you."

Mama said, exasperated, "Ibbie, I declare! You're acting just like one of the younguns! You'll have to wait and see." By this time Mama was feeling a bit guilty. This was turning out to be a mean trick, something Mama had never intended.

After Aunt Ibbie and Uncle John went home that Christmas Eve night, and everyone was in bed, Mama unwrapped the box, removed the shoes and placed Grandmama's tulip quilt inside. Christmas Day found Aunt Ibbie very touched by the gift, and at Mama's insistence, she accepted it. They hugged and cried as they stroked the quilt together and remembered previous Christmases when Grandmama was living.

But wait! Aunt Ibbie had a gift for Mama, too! It was a beautiful white apron with a pink ruffle around it and embroidery on the pocket. Mama wore the apron all that day. That was a very joyful Christmas.

Several months later, Mama revealed her Christmas prank. Aunt Ibbie said, "Why, you little rascal! I wondered why you would suddenly decide to part with Mama's quilt. And to think I sat up half the night making that apron for you! I'll get you back for it." We all began laughing, trying to anticipate what shenanigans would take place next.

Index

Are Flying Saucers Real?, 111
Aunt Ibbie, 70

Biosphere, The, 28
Box from the Heart, A, 23
Brain Dead, 126

Clothes Don't Make the Marriage, 57
Counting My Blessings, 87

Date to Remember, A, 61
Desert Storm, 135
Don't Get Your Dander Up, 107
Dozen Red Roses, A, 92

Edd Ragan Was a Fine Man, 147
Eight-year-old Forger, 82

First, Check It Out, 97
Food for Thought, 123

Good Deal, 127
Good Swap, 33
Graduation: A Time to Loosen the Ties, 48
Grammar Lesson, A, 79

Guardian Angel, 132

Hill Country Christmas, 139
Home, 36
Home for Christmas, 140
How High Is Up?, 20
How Old Is Old?, 84

I Believe in You, 41
I'm a Proud Member of the S.O.G. Club, 13
I Outwitted a Computer, 104
It's All in the Advertising, 74
It's Bad, 80

Just Behave, 35
Just Chasing Around, 78

Life's Changing Seasons, 18
Little Girl's Day, A, 30
Love Is Risky, 25
Lunch on the House, 109

Mama and Aunt Ibbie's Shenanigans, 151
Me and Mama and Shirley Temple, 43

Memories, 27
Migration, The, 67
My Slip Was Showing, 81

Numbers Are Good, 76

Old Folks Need a Keeper, 83
Old Man and the Boy, The, 17
One Letter Will Do, 73
One Life to Live, 88
Our Brothers Chock and Top, 71
Our Most Precious Gift, 142
Over the Hill?, 125

Papa, 38
Pen Name, 60
Please Pass the Syrup, 46
Prime the Pump, 130

Quilting, The, 65

Sacrifices, 56
"Sang Huntin'," 68
School Daze, 121
Sisters Will Be Sisters, 75

Special Lady, A, 86
Supreme Sacrifice, The, 49

Test of Time, The 53
Thanks, Mom!, 32
Think, Then Don't!, 113
Thou Shalt Not Judge, 98
Ticked Off, 101
Till Death Do Us Part, 54
Tomorrow May Never Be Mine, 94
Treasures of the Heart, 58
Tribute to a Great Singer, 85

Watch, The, 63
Way to a Mother-in-law's Heart, The, 21
We Can't Pick a Time to Be Sick, 115
We Must Be Careful, 105
Who's Counting?, 77
Who's Minding the Store?, 100
Wonderful Job, A, 16
Woodpile, The, 103

You Could Be Next, 128